HANGIN' WITH THE TRUTH

WATCH OUT FOR
THE "KING-QUEEN-ACE"

10/2018

Other Books by Mark Slade

GOING DOWN MAINE
A Novel

OF PAIN AND COFFEE
Sooths, Sayings & Soliloquies

SOMEONE'S STORY
Observations in Verse

HANGIN' WITH THE TRUTH

A Novel

Mark Slade

A Fortiori Enterprises
P.O. Box 671
Cloverdale, CA 95425
Email: **afortiorienterprises@yahoo.com**

First U.S. Print Edition October 2016

ISBN-13: 978-09885885-5-4
ISBN-10: 0-9885885-5-2

Printed in the United States of America

Photograph by Melinda Riccilli Slade
Photograph Copyright: A Fortiori Enterprises
www.marksladestudio.com

The Poem, HANGIN' WITH THE TRUTH, from "Someone's Story"
Reprinted Courtesy of A Fortiori Enterprises

Cover Design: Morgan Riccilli Slade
www.morganladestudio.com

For those whose "wild" takes them where they should not go.

"As often as you try an' make a bad idea good, it will still be a bad idea 'neath it."

Millie Mae Duncan
1876

HANGIN' WITH THE TRUTH

The historically bent tale of the Bandit Bob Slye

Historical Warning:
In various instances, historical facts, references, dates, events, names and places have been intentionally bent to accommodate this story

THE BANDIT BOB SLYE

ONE

Ol' Bob Slye was the apple of his mother's eye...
But, a bandit he would be.
Roaming the trails and towns, looking for unaware clowns.
And, picking the spoils from the likes of you and me.
He could slip a sheriff or a posse as quick as a hummingbird's flight.
Didn't matter if he rode after dark or struck in broad daylight.
For, the Bandit Bob Slye was the apple of his mother's eye...
And she taught him to be good at whatever he'd try...

WANTED
For Robbery & Skullduggery

THE BANDIT BOB SLYE

REWARD!

$1000.00

Bob Slye sat atop his sweating roan staring at the wanted poster nailed to a cottonwood tree next to the rutted stagecoach trail he'd been riding since before noon. *'Skullduggery,'* he thought. *'What the hell will they come up with next?'* It tickled him that this was what he was being accused of. "Skullduggery," he whispered aloud to his horse, sparking a bit of a crooked grin. He inched his mount closer and ripped the poster from the tree. The crude drawing of "The Bandit" wasn't even a close likeness. The only photograph that he'd ever had taken was at a photographer's studio back in Wichita, Kansas a few years back; the day he'd purchased a new Winchester Model 1873. Bob gave the only copy to his mother, Millie Mae, for her birthday and, being careful about not leaving any trail or details about himself behind, paid the photographer extra for the glass negative which he thoroughly smashed to smithereens, lest anyone try to match him up with some escapade he might have been involved in.

In actuality, Millie Mae had years previously reverted to her maiden name of Millie Mae Duncan, ever since what had happened with her husband, Jessup Slye, had besmirched the Slye name forever and always in her mind. She had encouraged her only son, Robert "Bob" Slye, to do the same; something he had done when the occasion suited the situation at hand.

The sun above was settling in on high noon. The Wells Fargo Stage would be passing through on its way north to Aberdeen. It wouldn't be a particularly difficult situation. Bob knew the territory fairly well, having grown up until the age of sixteen on a small sod house homestead in South Dakota. Not many in his profession operated along these particular roads and trails, because the travelers and supply wagons were usually of just the basic nature and not given to luxuries. But, once in a while, there would be the possibility of a gold or silver shipment in the wind or a well-off traveler aboard. Bob had caught this particular wind and waited amidst the clump of cottonwoods and scrub for the first sounds of hoofbeats off in the distance.

This would be an easy turn. Stagecoach drivers carried shotguns and sidearms but rarely used them, being that the stage line owners were not given to pay out any death benefits to their kin if they met with a lead-filled end.

Bob reached back into his saddlebag and pulled out the handkerchief wrapped black mustache and the small pyramid-shaped bottle of Egyptian Tenexine glue to affix it to his upper lip that was given to him by the traveling entertainer, one Mary Grace Doyle, after a rather wild coupling back in Deadwood, South Dakota. A time that Bob remembered fondly.

As a young man he was not familiar with the wild and wooly goings on in Deadwood, but only familiar with the tall tales told by the soldiers at nearby Fort Randall. And reading, and voraciously re-reading, the small collection of used Wild West dime novels he had picked up from some of the soldiers and squirreled away under his small log-framed bed; Bob had yearned to experience the temptations for himself. At sixteen years old, he went off to do just that and was not at all disappointed.

Bob pressed the large bushy mustache on and held it until it stuck. Then, he slipped on a pair of steel-rimmed dark sunglasses he'd picked up a month back from an out of work former Union soldier who was down on his luck. Bob had paid the young man a quarter-eagle gold piece for the oddity. Probably more than they were worth, but the man had told Bob that they were used in bright daylight to help shoot at the enemy. This information did not slip by Bob. Also, the fact that the darkened glass in the rims was green would help to cover his most telling physical characteristic, his cobalt blue eyes. Something not picked up on the wanted posters, as of yet. Bob waved off some annoying horseflies and listened intently for approaching hoofbeats.

Grace Doyle, a daughter of Ireland, was unique in many ways and he rather wished they'd been able to see more of each other before she'd gathered up her small troupe of theatrical players and moved along the frontier circuit.

Bob first caught sight of Grace at a large wood-fronted tent theater and saloon in Deadwood. The same year that George Armstrong Custer had arrived in the Black Hills with an expedition force of soldiers in search of a place to build a new fort. It was also the year that gold was reported to have been discovered by said soldiers. Bob had marveled at how Grace's small troupe of performers had transformed themselves into different characters. How the ventriloquist was able to throw his voice into the dummy seated on his knee. How the young woman contortionist twisted herself into a pretzel, thus exposing a certain area of her torso to her over-imaginative and over-intoxicated audience. Bob had also overheard a conversation as to how much she charged for a private demonstration after the show. True or not, this was a performance that was, above all, played out for the mainly male audiences, who were there to fantasize about what was going on beneath the exotic, cinched-up corsets, pink stockings and well-placed feather fans that teased and cajoled them into a drink buying frenzy of whistles, cheers and an occasional grab at the extremely voluptuous Grace and her ensemble of comely painted-up ladies, who sang and pranced around a wooden stage, at the far end of the large tent. All to the music of her raucous piano player, who pounded out everything from a sad Irish dirge to thumping, salacious, bawdy tunes.

Whatever Bob had expected Deadwood to be, seeing Grace belt out a wondrous Irish ballad brought his imagination to the boiling point. Watching from the nearest standing position he could get to the stage in the crowded, hot and smoky show and gambling den, Bob stood there transfixed by Grace - how she could entertain and manipulate the crowd of drunken miners and near-do-well rounders. He just had to meet her. And, meet her he did.

Young Bob had stationed himself outside the back entrance of the saloon theater tent and waited patiently in the semi-darkness for Grace to appear.

"Ma'am?" He'd asked her as she exited, after what had seemed to him an interminable passage of time.

"Yes?" Grace had answered in her throaty Irish brogue.

Nervously, Bob stammered out his reason for being there. "I was just wondering if I might have a moment of your time to talk about your show, ma'am, that's..."

Grace had immediately sparked to the freshness of the handsome young man standing there in front of her. It was seldom that she was confronted by anyone other than the sweat-covered, liquored-up rowdies who patronized her shows. She was probably not that many years older than Bob, but certainly experienced far beyond the young man's wildest dreams.

"Well, I think that could be arranged. What's your name?" she'd asked coyly.

"Bob, ma'am," he fumbled, "Robert... Robert Duncan, ma'am."

"Well, then, Robert Duncan. I have a bit of special *visitin'* to do. Why don't you meet me back here in about one hour and we'll find us some privacy in my room over t'that boarding house across the street to... talk about my show. How does that sound?"

Bob could feel his face redden even now, as he thought about that night and waited atop his horse for the stage to arrive... It was not quite the first time young Bob had been with a woman. Nevertheless, it was the first time he was initiated into such intense sensations that she commenced upon him that Grace Doyle would forever be present in his thoughts and dreams.

Bob had stayed in Deadwood for three days and four nights. All of them spent with Grace when she was finished with her *visitin'* and would return to her room at the boarding house, where they eventually did get around to having discussions of how she went about putting on her show. It would be a turning point for Bob. He was not going to settle for living out a life of drudgery on the frontier, trying to scratch out a measly existence from the South Dakota scrublands and struggling to survive the bone-chilling cold of the South Dakota winters. While he watched Millie Mae toil to prove up her homestead, according to U. S. Government requirements. There had to be a better way. He had already made a few secret forays into the world of a bandit. By using the old derringer pistol his father left behind, he procured some revenue and swag from some unsuspecting travelers. Moreover, just as he'd imagined from reading about other's exploits in the dime novels, they had been rather simple ventures, but no less exciting - unbeknownst to his mother, Millie Mae, of course. She had never used a strap on him, as his father had done, but knowing what her son was up to most certainly would have brought on a harsh discipline.

Between her passionate romps with young Bob, Grace taught him several techniques of the disguise that he had shown such a keen interest in. Not that she knew for sure what Bob's stock-in-trade would eventually turn out to be. Some things just go unspoken between the knowing. Although, she did have a history of her own and did ply a few specialties beyond singing Irish songs to raucous cowhands and gamblers.

As it worked out, in very short order, Bob developed into a first-class bandit and thought that, since there was only that one photograph of him in existence, changing up his appearance from time to time would add to protecting himself against being pursued after conducting one of his business ventures.

The stage was late Bob deduced from the solid gold pocket watch that came into his possession from one of his more lucrative larcenies. He pressed on the mustache to make sure it was in place. It wasn't the first time he'd used it. There were wanted posters out there with a sketch of a bandit with the same black mustache whom the jails were saving a cell for. He looked at the watch again. *Puzzling...*

One thing Bob prided himself on was his ability to plan the details of his conquests. He learned long ago that acting on an impulse did not always end with a successful result. His mother had told him on many an occasion as he was growing up, *"If'n your father had'a come home when he was supposed to, instead of headin' to a barroom or the gamblin', he'd'a been around for you to know."*

It seemed that Bob's father had been a philanderer and a chiseler who made off with a rich woman who was divorcing her husband – or, so she'd claimed. Seems the husband had other ideas and caught the two up short and left old man Slye in the hotel room to die. Which he did. Shortly thereafter, Millie Mae dropped her last name of Slye and reverted back to her maiden name of Duncan.

The only thing Bob had of his father's was the old derringer pistol that Jessup had brought back from fighting with the Rebs during the Civil War; being that he was originally from Alabama. Not even a tintype photograph existed. That's why Bob had made sure his mother had that photograph of himself, which she had framed and set on the bedside table of her tiny bedroom in the three room sod house on the Dakota homestead, where she still lived. Her mongrel stub-tailed dog Stubs, a fat gray mouser she called Buzzer because his purr sounded more like a snore, assorted layer hens, two goats, a horse of sorts who could still pull her buckboard, a stubborn mule named Dusty, along with occasional lambs for wool and chops filled out her menagerie. Often there was a cow or two, depending on when she'd slaughter a dried up milker to sell to the Army cooks at Fort Randall or to other homesteaders out on the frontier. She'd tried raising a few hogs, but they ate up more than they brought in revenue, so she slaughtered two, smoked the meat and sold the others off. The homestead didn't bring in all that much as far as actual cash money was involved, but she got by with bartering the milk, eggs, churned butter and whatnot. And, being a sure shot with her old single-fire Army issue Bridesburg Model 1861 musket rifle, she could get herself a hare, wild turkey, grouse or other edible varmint whenever necessary. Fortunately, a spring bubbled up beneath a small pond on the land that supplied more than enough water for herself, her animals and the vegetable garden she plowed behind Dusty and tended every season. Although the little sunfish that spawned in the pond were not much more than a snack, they did add to fertilizing the garden, when they were caught, dried and mixed with chicken droppings and other animal and food waste. As far as Millie Mae was concerned, nothing on the homestead was to be squandered. She had even ventured after the bullfrogs in the pond, but thought better of it when she thought about missing their familiar croaks at night.

His horse's ears twitched and Bob felt the roan's body tense under him. He'd already stashed his prized *Boss of the Plains* hat, along with his usual black tailored gentleman's duds, back a distance from the road in the brush having replaced them with a sweat-stained trail shirt, rumpled pants and a wool worker's cap on his head, covering most of his cropped black hair. He purposely hadn't shaved for several days, adding to the description that he knew the stagecoach drivers and their passengers would relate to the nearest sheriff. He'd shave after his business was done.

Being clean-shaven, without the mustache and wearing his distinctive *Boss of the Plains* hat would alter the direction of anyone who might try to pursue "The Bandit."

His horse had heard the hoofbeats of the approaching stage before he had. Now, the distinct rumbling of the steel-rimmed wooden-spoked wheels approached from the distance. Bob reached back, drew his Winchester '73 out of its scabbard and locked in a round.

If all went as planned, and for Bob it usually did, the operation would be over almost before it had begun. He reached forward and patted his horse's neck to keep him calm. They'd been together going on three years now, but the moment of execution never failed to excite the animal.

Conducting business on a stage route was fairly routine. Bob had felled a medium sized tree across the rutted stage road about fifty yards back from where he was waiting amongst the trees. He would wait until he heard the drivers frantically shout as they pulled up the team of horses. Then, taking advantage of the confusion, he would suddenly spur the roan out onto the road like a coiled spring and fire his Winchester into the air.

All went as he had planned. Except for one

problem. As the lead driver patiently explained, "We've already been hit, 'bout ten mile back. Took the strongbox and everythin' off the travelers we got on board. Fleeced us good."

Bob pondered the situation for a moment, making sure that neither the lead driver nor the guard riding shotgun made a sudden move. They didn't. Bob didn't speak. He never did. The less he gave over of himself, the less the law had to go on.

After a long moment, he signaled with his Winchester for the stage to pass on by. The driver nodded and moved the reins over the team to his left. The four-horse rig turned the stage off the roadway and slowly moved around the felled tree. Bob watched and made sure he wasn't being hoodwinked. He didn't see a strongbox under the driver's seat or any luggage strapped to the coach. The boot flap was open and the space empty of contents. The wide, frightened eyes of the two women and the gentleman inside told him that the driver had told the truth.

As the driver clucked and reined the team back up onto the roadway, he glanced over at Bob sitting astride the roan. "It t'was a woman who stopped us..." Bob noticeably tensed. "...and, she was as nasty a little creature as I've ever come across! A real rattler!"

Bob nodded slowly. The driver nodded back, then slapped the reins over the team and moved on down the road.

A woman... Bob rolled the words over in his mind, as he waited for the stage to disappear around the bend... *A woman...*

TWO

But, what Ol' Bob Slye didn't see coming,
was a rival bandit who possessed a much different
style of cunning.
For he wasn't a he, you see.
She was a she – Woe-is-me...

Bob didn't usually make camp in the wild often, preferring to take a room in a nearby hotel or boarding house after depositing his newly acquired loot in a pre-selected hiding place; knowing that no one would suspect someone of robbing a stage to then show up in town. But, this time he felt that sticking around the area might be useful. No telling if this *woman* bandit had hightailed it far and away or was waiting for another opportunity to strike again. Something Bob would hasten not to try, but he'd seen others make just that greedy mistake.

He rode back through the woods to a creek he had passed over on the way to his rendezvous with the stage. Dismounting, he led the horse to the water and took out a cloth towel from a saddlebag. When the horse was finished drinking down his thirst, Bob dipped the towel into the stream and then proceeded to wash away the white stage makeup marking he'd applied to the animal's forehead to, once again, throw off the description of the bandit that he knew would be given to the law. Bob chuckled to himself as he removed the fake black mustache and pondered what his next wanted poster would look like. Another reason to be glad he'd met up with the traveling performer Grace Doyle.

Bob settled onto his oilcloth bedroll and read from one of his dog-eared dime novels by the flickering light of a small campfire to help while away the time.

As a youngster, Bob had imagined himself as the main character in the dime novels he'd picked up at Fort Randall. He was always the hero or, better yet, the villain who got away with the spoils. Or, maybe, *Seth Jones* in *The Captives of the Frontier* by Edward S. Ellis.

Learning to read had been quite easy for Bob. Fortunately, Millie Mae was very strict on him to listen to her read passages from her Bible and, eventually, teach him the words that made up her favorite Psalms. But, it was Miss Marjorie Lundergan who had given him the most schooling out on the Dakota plains. She was a trained teacher from Ohio who had taken advantage of the new homestead laws and had established a one-room sod schoolhouse on her land. It was common knowledge that men far outnumbered women on the frontier. If a woman didn't want to end up a spinster, she would be much in demand if she laid claim to a homestead; which Miss Lundergan had done. Quite fortunate for young Bob because he had thrived in that little sod walled schoolroom.

Miss Lundergan had a word box whereby she took out words painted on pieces of wood and spread them out on the floor for the several frontier children to make into a sentence. Bob never failed at these tests and was forever grateful for having been able to walk the five miles each way for his daily lessons. He'd marveled at the large book of maps she had, showing that there was much more to see beyond his mother's South Dakota homestead. And, as it turned out, much more to see of Miss Lundergan, when she had insisted that he stay on a bit longer after the others had departed for the day.

The waiting through the night and part of the next day was for naught. No one, except for a rabbit – which became breakfast – and a deer or two came within sight of Bob's camp. Finally, as the sun began to roll up overhead, Bob stripped down and scrubbed up in the cool running creek. He then, letting his body dry off in the warmth of the sun filtering down through the trees, retrieved his shaving gear from a saddlebag. He gently set the small Chinese shaving mirror box in the crotch of a low-slung tree branch, then sharpened the Skinner Warranted Straight Razor on the Emerson Elastic Razor Strap he carried in the saddlebag. Both of which he had relieved from a well-off traveler during his first year of officially becoming a professional bandit in the eyes of the law. After applying a lather of goat's milk soap, he expertly whipped off the deceptive scruff, brushed his teeth with the bristle brush and reminded himself to pick up a new jar of Dr. Peabody's Toothpaste when he could.

Washed, shaven and dried off, he quickly slipped into his gentleman's shirt and pants, adjusted his *Boss of the Plains* hat, scratched out the remnants of his having been there and rode off toward Deadwood; where he would replenish a few necessities. And, get the lay of the land, with regard to deciding what and where his next target would be. He was also in need of a card game and a warm woman. It had been a while.

Quite some time had slipped by since Bob had experienced this part of the South Dakota Territory. However, the memories of his first trek to Deadwood were still fresh in his mind. As he rode down the crowded, rutted dirt street, weaving around the horse piss pools and dung deposits, he came upon the place where he'd first laid eyes on and experienced the delicacies of the Irish entertainer, Grace Doyle. He reined up the roan and took in the view before him.

The large wood-fronted tent that housed the saloon and theater was gone. In its place was being erected a more permanent two and three story building that he found out would be the home of the new Gem Theater. According to its owner, one Iowa born Ellis Alfred Swearengen, all forms of gambling and entertainment would be on exhibition to tempt and entice a thirsty clientele. Swearengen, he learned, reigned over his brood of prostitutes with an iron fist. If any of them got out of line, there would be hell to pay.

Bob sighed, as he imagined that he might once again lie beside the wonderful Grace Doyle, if she, by chance, should play the new Gem Theater and he was to hear about it.

Bob turned his horse away and rode on down the street in search of a livery. He was amazed at how fast Deadwood had grown since he first set foot there. More people crisscrossing all about. More horses. More men with guns strapped to their belts. More stores selling gold mining supplies. More gambling saloons and brothels. More oxen pulled wagons heading in, out and through Deadwood. And, more pools of piss.

While many of the frontier towns were similar to each other - mostly built up on or near the rivers, cattle trails or a railhead of the day - Deadwood was much different. The town literally exploded into existence. Word had spread like wildfire far and wide that there was gold in the surrounding Black Hills and badlands. Some towns had law. Some did not. This one did. Bob had noticed the Deadwood Sheriff's Office set out prominently as he'd entered the town, reminding those who ventured in that there might be consequences if one should run afoul of the law. That could only mean that the ruling citizens of Deadwood had bought and paid for their protection, which suited Bob just fine; because it meant that - being a stranger - he probably would not have to draw down on anyone, if he kept his powder dry, which he usually tried to do. However, one thing was clear. This was a wild, untamed frontier where anything and anyone could be had for a price. A great deal of the town's income came from eating, drinking, gambling, cheating and houses of ill-repute. Slick assayers of gold abounded. Carpetbaggers of all stripes were ready to fleece the unwitting out of their newfound nuggets. Luckily, for Bob, he was well-schooled at spotting the professional flimflammers. After all, he was one himself. One of the best, as far as he was concerned.

The stable boy at the livery, where Bob paid to put up his horse, directed him to Nuttal & Mann's Saloon on Main Street, when he asked where he could get a room, a drink, a good steak, a card game and a woman, in that order.

Having only stayed in her room at the rooming house those remarkable few days with Grace Doyle, Bob knew very little about Deadwood, except for its far-flung reputation and stories retold along other routes, and in some of the dime novels he had read. He also made sure the boy knew how serious a situation could arise if his saddle and tack were mishandled in any way. And, that there was an extra four bits in it if he cleaned them up, kept an eye on them and made sure his roan was brushed down, fed and cared for.

As Bob entered Nuttal & Mann's Saloon and Hotel, carrying his Winchester '73 with his saddlebags slung over his shoulder, he first sized up the crowded, smoke-filled hotel bar where the card tables were at full tilt. The piano player was plunking out *Sweet Evelina* under the din. The painted ladies for hire could have been there or anywhere. They all looked the same, all rouged-up and looking to make their quotas. Bob didn't return their sultry glances. He wasn't ready for that, as yet.

First Bob asked for a room. It never mattered that there wasn't one available. There was always one or two held back for a higher payer. He paid and got his room. Upstairs and down a dark hallway. Mostly away from the noise... mostly.

He set his saddlebags down by the hat rack next to the door of the musty, dark room. A small chest of drawers was set beneath a painting of a plump, nude prostitute lying seductively draped over a lounge. Bob poured some water from a metal pitcher into a small ceramic washbasin. As he rinsed off his hands and face, he thought about the ride in and how he passed the luggage and the empty strongbox from the stage holdup strewn on the roadway... *a woman...*

"Damn!" he said aloud, "Dammit!"

Growing up near the frontier Fort Randall, just south of the Missouri River in South Dakota, with only his mother to keep an eye on him had its benefits. Bob had been taken under the wings of the head cook at the fort, Jasper Spence, who sometimes bought a chicken or goat from Millie Mae; and Master Sergeant William H. Bartholomew, who had taken a liking to Bob's mother, and she to him, on a friendship basis - or the story they let be. Both Spence and Bartholomew had contributed to his education. The cook by teaching young Bob how to live off the land, to count cards, and deal from the bottom of the deck. Master Sergeant Bartholomew instructed him how to be a marksman with a pistol and a rifle and, more importantly to young Bob, he introduced him to several of the women-of-pleasure outside the fort, who made it their business to service the men in the service of their country. All unbeknownst to Bob's mother, of course.

All of this education came in handy, as young Bob began to wander ever further away from the small homestead and develop his skills in his chosen field of endeavor - to relieve owners of their cash, valuables and other gratuities that his targets might offer up under the threat of extinction. Something that Bob never carried out on an innocent mark, but was at the ready to do so, lest one of them objected to the incursion with an equal threat to Bob's life and limb.

Freshened up from the ride into Deadwood, Bob headed back down to the main bar and card room. He would go to the bar, order up a whiskey and a steak as he quietly sized up the card games going on at the different tables. Gambling was a forever game on the Western Frontier. Meaning that there was a game going on somewhere *forever.*

He watched closely as two faro games were operating at two tables close to the long bar. Bob was an experienced faro player and winner, because he was so adept at counting the cards that flew out of the dealer's card box. However, he was also adroit at spotting a gaffed cheating box and knew immediately that these two *Bucking the Tiger* games were not for him. They were both rigged, as were most of the frontier faro games. In fact, it was said that there wasn't a fair faro game to be found anywhere in the land.

"A sucker's game," Bob would tell anyone who would show an interest in playing. But, rarely did anyone listen to his warnings. This particular game of chance had the fast pace, easy rules and the potential for a high payoff that was too much of an attraction for the miners, speculators, cowboys, gamblers and the thirsty drovers who poured into the frontier bars and brothels looking for action after a long cattle drive.

Bob's early decision to avoid the faro tables came when he was just eighteen years old and found himself celebrating his birthday by seating himself down at a game near Pierre, South Dakota. His ante in with a five-dollar gold piece was nearly depleted within three quick hands. It was Bob's learned skill at counting cards that told him there was something peculiar about the *Banker's Box*. A quicker eye might spot that there just might be more than one card lifted to the top of the dealer's tray. What Bob did, instead of causing the usual row of accusing the dealer of cheating – always a lost cause and an excuse for a night in jail and a hefty fine being that the local law was part and parcel of the game's shenanigans - was to slowly reach down into his boot and lift out the old Civil War derringer and point it under the table at the dealer's crotch and pull back on the hammer. It was both the simultaneous *click* and Bob's silent, steely stare into the dealer's eyes that told the cheater that Bob knew that the dealer knew that Bob meant business. Bob expected that the next several hands would not only win Bob back his illegally gotten losses, but would also top them off with a reward of sorts for not sending a lead slug blasting into the offender's precious bollocks.

"You in?" the gentleman whose deal it was directed at Bob, who was standing near the poker table contemplating whether to take up the one empty chair left.

"Well, yessir, don't mind if I do," Bob answered pleasantly and pulled back the chair opposite the present dealer, who sat with his back to the wall. Bob anted the minimum bet and waited for his cards.

"The name's Hickok, sir. James Hickok," the gambler said, introducing himself. "And, this here's Jack 'Broken Nose' McCall," Hickok said nodding at the gambler seated next to him. "Poor Jack ain't doin' so well tonight. Are'ya, Jack?" Hickok chuckled as he finished dealing out the poker hand to all.

Bob looked up from the cards he had been dealt and set out three face down. Hickok squinted noticeably at Bob and dealt him three new cards. "You didn't say who you might be," Hickok directed to Bob, as he also tossed down three cards of his own and deftly dealt himself three more.

"Robert Duncan from down Fort Randall way," Bob answered as he looked at the pot in the center of the table. Not a bad size to take if he'd wanted to, but small enough to pass on, which he did by nonchalantly tossing his cards facedown toward Hickok, letting the others play out the hand with Hickok eventually dragging in the winnings.

An angry Jack McCall flipped his cards right toward Hickok in disgust and tossed the remainder of his whisky down his gullet. Hickok paid McCall no mind and expertly shuffled the deck and placed it down on the table for Bob to cut.

"Haven't seen you a'fore 'round these parts, I don't believe, Mister Duncan. You here lookin' to strike it rich in the hills?"

Bob watched as Hickok smoothly dealt out the new hands. "Nossir. I'm not in the mining business." Bob offered no more and picked up his last card. It was a good hand. He'd need only one card to fill it out.

Bob had made it a personal rule of his to never start off by winning the first hands in a poker game. It also gave him a chance to mentally file away as many cards as he could to give him an advantage toward the end of the deck.

"How're the women here?" he asked to no one at the table in particular.

A mustached, unshaven drover seated next to Bob answered up with, "Well, this place has the usual throw-downs and diddlers, as far as that goes. One ain't no better or worse than t'other."

"Have enough liquor in-ya, they all look good," another joked, eliciting a gurgle of laughs from everyone except Jack McCall.

"Like to have branded that little bitch who took us last night, I'll tell you that much," added a tall, lanky traveling carpetbagger across the table.

The comment piqued Bob's interest, as he contemplated the new draw in his hand and tossed in a medium bet. "How's that?"

"Well," the carpetbagger added, "this little half-pint sets down at our game last night and starts right in winnin' near every hand right off. We all thought he was a man until she starts talkin' and it dawned on us that the little shite was a damned woman!"

"S'right," chimed in the drover. "An' when this regular gambler called her on how she might be palming cards, she drew down on'im faster than a rattler strikin' a gopher."

"Really?" uttered Bob. "She from around these parts?" Bob asked almost as an afterthought, as he contemplated his cards.

"Never seed'er a'fore, but I heard that a stage was held up out on the trail by a woman. At least, that's the story comin' back here."

"Kind'a hard to believe less'n you'd seen her draw a Colt .45 in your face," added the carpetbagger.

"Where's she at now?" Bob asked and upped his bet substantially.

"Gone with the wind, I suspect."

Hickok dropped one card and dealt himself another. "Wished I'd've been here to see that," he said with a chuckle.

Jack McCall angrily blurted out, "Are we gonna sit around chitchattin' or play the goddamned cards?!"

The betting circled again and Bob folded his hand. The carpetbagger won the pot and, once again, Jack McCall uttered a curse and shouted for a painted lady to get him a whiskey.

Hickok passed the deck to the winning carpetbagger and uttered to McCall, "Say there, Jack, why not call it a night'n'come back tomorrow when you're fresh."

"Fuck you!" Jack mumbled with utter belligerence.

Hickok shrugged and anted in. "Suit yourself."

The game circled several more times until Bob held the deal on a small pot win. Bob expertly shuffled the cards, let them be cut and easily slipped the deals out to the table of gamblers. This did not go unnoticed by Hickok. "That's a pretty nice dealin' hand you've got there. You a professional?" he squinted at Bob as he asked with a bit of a challenge.

"Nossir, just was taught by a soldier when I was growin' up near Fort Randall. Don't get to play much except when I come upon a town now and again."

The pot grew to the point that McCall became very agitated and started noticeably grinding his teeth. He was cleaned out and couldn't make the bet. He told Hickok to make him a loan and that he'd 'even up' in the morning. Hickok declined and told him to quit and offered him a few coins. "Go get somethin' to eat, Jack, and go home and sleep it off!"

McCall violently threw in his cards, shoved back his chair and wobbled to a standing position. "Fuck you, Hickok! Fuck you all!" he blurted out. With that, Jack "Broken Nose" McCall stumbled to the front door and, as he pushed through to leave, shouted out one more curse at Hickok, "Piss-on-you-Wild-Bill-Hickok! You're nothin'! You hear me? You ain't nothin'!" Then he disappeared into the night.

Bob didn't let on that McCall's last utterance made an impression on him. He had previously deduced that the *James* Hickok seated with his back to the wall was, most certainly, the infamous Wild Bill Hickok, who had thrilled young Bob with his sharpshooter exploits in the *Beadle and Company* dime novels he had read so fervently. He just calmly dealt out the rest of the cards and in the end raked in the large pot by letting the others know with his eyes that he did, indeed, hold the winning hand.

Bob took out his gold pocket watch, looked at the time and politely excused himself from the game, taking his winnings with him, but not before tossing a generous gratuity to the hostess who was servicing their table and suggesting to the others with a grin, "Never trust a woman with a .45 Colt strapped to her hip."

The poker players chuckled begrudgingly and nodded in their defeat. Hickok raised two fingers to Bob to hold up for a moment. "Sir, you will be back tomorrow, I suspect?" It was more of a demand than a question, even though Hickok had a grin on his face. Bob started to answer. Hickok spoke over him, "Fort

Randall, you say? I know it well. That cook, Jasper Spence, can't grill a grouse for shit, but can cook up a real good venison stew; I'll tell you that..." Bob tried not to show any reaction to the mention of Jasper Spence. "Tell you what," Hickok continued, "there's a damned good cook over at the Grand Central Hotel name of Aunt Lou. You go over there for your breakfast and tell'er I sent you. She'll fix you up good. Best food west of the Mississippi, ain't that right gentlemen?" The others mumbled their agreements.

Bob nodded and touched the brim of his *Boss of the Plains* hat and headed toward the stairs to the rooms above.

Back in his room, Bob ignored the groans of bodily satisfaction coming through the thin wall of the room next door. His mind was not taken up with thoughts of bedding a woman of pleasure. His brain was throbbing with the idea of this woman bandit who could rob a stage, fleece a poker table all in the same day, and then disappear like a puff of pipe smoke.

One of the reasons Bob was successful at what he did was because greed was put aside long ago by the examples set out by his mother, Millie Mae. *"Greed will choke the life out of you. The more you eat from the Horn of Plenty, the fatter you get until you explode from your gluttony."*

In fact, Bob rarely set foot in the same town again until enough time had gone by that neither the locals nor transients would remember him from being there before. He did, however, always tend to observe the local law and make note of what kind of force they might bring down on anyone unfortunate enough to come up against it.

Deadwood, South Dakota was a product of the Gold Rush that had roared onto a Sioux Reservation, when the news that George Armstrong Custer's expedition regiment had discovered gold in the Black Hills had spread hither and yon. However, as far as the Federal Government was concerned, the town was very much an illegal assemblage of prospectors, profiteers, gamblers and ne'er-do-wells looking to make a killing from golden nuggets or just killing for the hell of it. And, commerce being what it was, the government tended to look the other way in such matters.

Until Bob had inadvertently heard about the interloping woman bandit, he had intended to do a little bit of fleecing of his own to make up for losing out on his planned stage heist. But, now he started to think about altering his plan. He needed more information about just who this mysterious female was and where she'd emanated from. To Bob, it was becoming personal. It wasn't that he had any kind of deed to rob in the territory. There were others who were in the same trade; notably, the notorious Big Nose George Parrott, who the stories about the territory alleged, was not a man to go up against. However, they all tended to keep out of each other's way and operated under an unwritten code that said one should not interlope onto another's area, if it was known that a certain bandit was operating thereabouts. Of course, this rule was not always adhered to. But mostly, it helped in avoiding getting yourself shot up by a competitor. Up until then, Bob had never heard of a woman robbing a stagecoach. And, *his* stagecoach to boot!

Bob had trouble getting to sleep and finally awoke long after high noon, as the sun streamed through his window that overlooked the alley below.

Although the Grand Central Hotel itself would have trouble living up to its imposing name, the meal of fresh eggs, ham steak, just-made biscuits and gravy, served up with freshly brewed coffee, was the best he could remember.

"How you like my cookin'?"

Bob looked up at the strong looking black woman refilling his coffee mug.

"I have to tell you, Miss... ah...

"Lucretia Marchbanks," she interjected with a firm smile, "but I'm called Aunt Lou by the folks around here."

"Well, Aunt Lou, I have to tell you I will remember this day for the rest of my life because of your cooking, I can assure you. Mister Hickok was right about recommending that I stop in here." Bob said with the utmost sincerity.

A look of melancholy flickered in her dark eyes. "Sad to see him like this... Such a gentleman..."

"Ma'am?"

She brushed off her remark, "S'nothin'," and quickly brightened. "Then I expect to see you again, sir," she said with a firmness that she meant what she'd said.

"Well, if I'm ever around these parts again, you can bet on it. Thank you very much for your hospitality, ma'am."

"Just passin' through then?"

"Yes, ma'am."

"I was thinkin' you don't look like a prospector, what with that *Boss of the Plains* hat and that Colt Peacemaker you're packin'. Must be a gambler, I'd say."

Bob chuckled a bit. "As it is, I write stories about the Western Frontier," Bob volunteered with his planned occupational answer to anyone who might ask.

"Oh, I see. Then, maybe you'll make me famous!" Aunt Lou said brightly.

"Well, from what I hear, you're already famous there, Miss Marchbanks." Lucretia Marchbanks' laugh was infectious, as she turned to fill another customer's coffee mug. "Well, I expect I am a bit famous for my plum puddin', that's for sure. You should try some."

"I sure wish I had the time to oblige you, ma'am, but this being the second day of August, and already coming up to mid-afternoon, I've overstayed my welcome as it is."

"Suit yerself. You don't know what you're missin'." She then headed for the kitchen.

Bob paid up for his late breakfast and started for the front door. "Wait up there, sir," came Lucretia Marchbanks' command from behind him. She approached and handed him a small lunch tin.

"What's this?"

Her face, etched from years of guts, glory and gumption, crinkled with a big smile as she handed him the closed lunch tin. "This'll tide you over a bit out there on the trail to wherever it is you're headed. Besides, you have the spark in'ya, I can tell."

Bob accepted the tin and slipped his hand into his pocket. Lucretia held up her hand. "I won't accept payment, sir."

"Well, let me shake your hand then." She offered her hand, which Bob took firmly in his and smiled knowingly at her expression when she felt the quarter gold piece he pressed into her palm. Then, he touched his index finger to the brim of his *Boss of the Plains* hat and, with a grin and a nod, was gone...

"T'was Mister Hickok's family that helped many of my people get North durin' the war..."

"I see... I didn't know that, Miss Marchbanks..."

"Not many folks do... But, it's worth the tellin'."...

Bob walked over to the Wells Fargo Office, taking care to avoid getting as little mud as possible on his black genuine calfskin boots.

The spring doorbell tinkled above his head as he entered the small board and timber stage office. A ticket master came out of the back room and automatically went toward his desk as if to book a passenger. He was a dwarfish man of about four foot tops. "Stage should be here soon," he said as he routinely hiked himself up onto his oak desk chair with a thick pillow on it to boost his height.

Bob stood in front of the man's desk. "I'm not here for the stage. I was just wondering if you had any information on the robbery yesterday."

"No. Nothin' yet."

"Heard it was a woman bandit," Bob said, smiling.

"Well, that's the story comin' back."

"Curious."

"What's your interest, mister?"

"I'm a writer of stories of the Western Frontier," Bob replied, keeping the story of his occupation going. "I heard about it over at Nuttal & Mann's last night. Thought there might be something I might look into for a story."

"Oh, well, that's all I've heard so far. You might ask over at the sheriff's office on down the end of the boardwalk, across the street. Sheriff O'Banyon. But, be warned, he's a nasty fella and doesn't cotton to strangers much."

"Thanks for the warning," Bob smiled and touched his index finger to the brim of his hat.

The main street of Deadwood was a thick sludge of muck and ruts that was consistent with the constant passage of horses, oxen, mules and cattle that trafficked in and out of town nearly twenty-four hours a day. Several wide planks were interspersed that crisscrossed the street to offer some respite from the muck. Bob chose to use them as opposed to dodging the dung.

"Where would I find Sheriff O'Banyon?" Bob asked the dozing man in the chair just outside the sheriff's office.

The tall, rather lanky chap unfolded his arms, uncovering a star badge pinned to his coarsely woven, oft-sewn shirt. He squinted into the sun, trying to get a good look at who was asking. "Who needs to know?" came the question in a somewhat spitting nature.

"Name's Bob Duncan, Sheriff." Bob answered and offered his hand. It wasn't taken.

"Deputy Sheriff."

"I see. Well, is the sheriff about?"

The deputy eyed Bob up and down. "Inside with the missus."

Bob stepped toward the door to the office.

"I wouldn't if'n I was you."

Bob stopped just short of opening the door.

"They been goin' at it for a while now. You might get caught in the crossfire." The deputy chuckled at his own joke, spat a slurp of chaw juice up and out onto the muddy street.

There was a definite sound of a sharp slap to someone's face from inside, then the unmistakable curse of a man, "You fuckin' bitch! No one does that to me!" With that, a woman dressed in a white frilly store-bought frock, came crashing out through the partially opened door and right into Bob's arms. Stunned, he quickly tried to untangle himself from the distraught woman, but not before the burly, imposing form of Sheriff Jack O'Banyon stood framed in the doorway.

Bob quickly set the woman apart from himself. The sheriff grabbed her by both arms and shoved her headlong off the boardwalk and into the horse-mucked street.

"You bastard! You sick bastard! I know what you do with those whores you bring into that jail cell!" The woman cried out through a burst of tears.

Sheriff O'Banyon snorted back with a sneering grin, "You get yourself back to the house woman, an' don't come out less'n I says so, or I'll see that you go right back to the Gem whorehouse where I found you! Now get your scrawny ass out of here!"

As the sheriff's wife started to lift herself out of

the muck, Bob noticed that she was not scrawny at all. In fact, her left breast was quite full and pink, being that it was fully exposed as a result of the violent tumble she had taken. Bob watched her stumble to her horse drawn buckboard next to the hitching post and climb up onto the seat.

The sheriff admonished her, "Tuck that droopin' udder of yours in 'fore this gentleman here messes his long johns!" Then he laughed cruelly, as she stuffed her breast into the front of her ruined dress and reined the horse and buckboard away and up the muddy street.

"Once a whore, always a whore," the sheriff uttered, then to Bob he snapped, "What's your business? I'm assuming you're here to see me and not my deputy there."

"Yessir, the name's Duncan, Robert Duncan. I have a few questions about the stage robbery yesterday." Bob offered his hand to the sheriff. It wasn't taken.

"You from the newspapers?" the sheriff grumbled.

"Well, not really."

"What the hell's that supposed to mean?"

"I write stories about the Wild West for magazines and books back East."

"Oh, is that right?" the sheriff smirked sarcastically.

"Yessir, and I was just wondering if you'd heard anything about the bandit that..."

"A goddamned woman, supposed to be!" the sheriff interrupted and laughed at the absurdity, as he headed inside, leaving the door open for Bob to follow.

"Yes, so I heard over at Nuttal & Mann's last

night and thought there might be a good story there," Bob said, as he entered the sheriff's office after O'Banyon.

The sheriff circled around to his desk chair, sat his large frame into it and extended his boots up onto his desk. Bob couldn't miss the large case of rifles and pistols arranged behind him. He also noticed that the sheriff sported a shiny gold eye tooth that reflected in the light as he grinned at him. O'Banyon nonchalantly picked up a leather English riding crop that looked to be well used and stained with what could be dried blood...

"Well, mister... what'd you say your name is?" O'Banyon asked as he absently tapped the riding crop on his desk.

"Robert Duncan."

"Well, Robert Duncan, I probably don't know any more than you or anyone else."

"Okay... well, then... it's just that I've never heard of a woman bandit before and..."

"Where you from, Bob? They call you Bob, right?" the sheriff interjected over Bob, who was a bit taken off guard.

"Well, um, from all over, I guess. I travel quite a bit."

"Originally. Where you from originally?"

"Nearby Fort Randall."

O'Banyon nodded. "Nice boots you're sportin' there. Calfskin?" the sheriff asked smiling.

"Ah, yessir..."

"That a *Boss of the West*?" he asked, indicating Bob's hat.

"Boss of the *Plains*, sir," Bob corrected.

"Right-right... *Boss of the Plains...*" the sheriff mused with a slanted grin.

"Yessir, it is." Bob answered with a bit of pride.

O'Banyon nodded toward Bob's right hip. "That's a Peacemaker, ain't it?"

"Yessir."

"Army issue?" He asked, eyeing Bob. Then right over Bob's beginning of an answer, "So, you were in the U.S. Army there, Bob?"

"Well, nossir. As I said, I was raised up near Fort Randall and I..."

The sheriff darkened a bit. "That-there story writtin' game must pay pretty good."

Bob got the gist of where the sheriff was headed. "It pays when I deliver, but I do fortify my gains at the tables when I'm in a town."

"Ha! Thought so! A gambler!" O'Banyon nearly shouted and slapped the riding crop down hard on his desk with a bit too much glee.

"I wouldn't say that... I get lucky once in a while."

"Hell, I'd say you got pretty lucky last night over there at Nuttal & Mann's. Took some of the boys for most of what they brought to the table, I hear."

"Luck, pure luck."

The sheriff paused and eyed Bob, then grinned his gold-toothed grin. "Yeah... we all get lucky once in a while, don't we, Bob. Heard old Wild Bill was quite impressed with your dealin'." It wasn't a question.

Bob decided his time with the sheriff was best ended. "Well, thank you for your time, Sheriff, I should..."

O'Banyon shouted over Bob, "Hey, Pignuts! Get

your sorry cockle-burred ass in here!" The deputy charged into the office. O'Banyon leveled him with, "I thought I told you to swamp out that back cell! It fuckin' stinks with vomit and shit in there from last night!"

The deputy looked wild-eyed. "I was gonna, but you and the missus was..."

The sheriff leaned forward over his desk and fingered the riding crop as he admonished the deputy in a menacing monotone, "I-don't-give-a-fistful-of-goose-shit-who's-here... I tell you to do somethin' you do it, less'n you wanna go back to dumpin' spittoons at a stinkin' Chinese whorehouse. Now, get your ass in there, you piece of dog shit, 'fore I change my mind... And, chuck that flea-bitten drunk whore outta there now!" O'Banyon suddenly shouted and slammed the riding crop down hard on the wooden desk.

"Yessir," the deputy mumbled and skulked away toward the hallway to the cells.

Bob stood there for a moment, then eased toward the door.

"Fuckin' slim pickin's around here goddammit," the sheriff mumbled, then he suddenly brightened and grinned at Bob. "Hey there, Bob," the sheriff said evenly, "you gonna make me famous?"

"Sir?" Bob answered quizzically.

"You gonna put me in one of your Wild West stories?" There was an element of danger in the sheriff's tone.

Bob chuckled a bit nervously, "I'll see what I can do, sir."

"You do that, Bob Duncan. You do that. Now,

be on your way, I got work to do here. We got two hangin's comin' up this week."

Bob touched his finger to his *Boss of the Plains* hat and made his exit.

Out on the front walkway, Bob watched a team of oxen slowly slog by hauling a prairie schooner with a family aboard heading north. If nothing else, the conversation with Sheriff O'Banyon, as well as seeing how he had shoved his wife down into the horse muck and how he treated his deputy, told Bob that it might be a good idea not to become a familiar face around Deadwood, South Dakota.

As he turned to walk up the wood plank walkway, the front door swung open with a bang and the deputy emerged roughly gripping the arm of a rather petit woman, who had obviously had a bad night. She held the front of her torn dress up over her chest as best she could, although, not that successfully. Her badly smeared makeup told Bob that she, most certainly, was a prostitute who had been arrested for who knows what and had spent the night back in one of O'Banyon's cells being abused and subjected to who knows what else. Possibly, the reason the sheriff's wife had been so upset.

The deputy brushed by Bob and forcefully shoved the woman forward, almost knocking her down. "Scat!" he ordered. She turned. Glared at him and spat on the wooden walkway before she scurried away from the sheriff's office. The deputy headed back to the office door, but stopped before he entered and turned to Bob. He uttered, "Otis Thigpen."

"Sir?" Bob questioned.

"The name's Otis Thigpen, in case you was wonderin'." With that, he disappeared inside.

Still holding the small lunch tin that Lucretia Marchbanks had given him, Bob took out the gold pocket watch from his vest pocket and looked at the time. He would have to get a move on if he were to get any traveling done before sundown. He then headed back to the Nuttal & Mann's Saloon and Hotel to retrieve his saddlebags and Winchester '73 rifle.

Back in the room, Bob decided not to shave; thinking that he would be needing his scruffy looking face and black mustache in the not too distant future. He did, however, open the small lunch tin and, as he'd already suspected, it was filled with Aunt Lou's famous plum pudding. He put the tin in a saddlebag, then gathered up the rest of his things and headed back downstairs.

As he started across the saloon toward the front door, a voice from the night before called out to him, "Hey, there!" It was the gambler, Wild Bill Hickok, standing at the bar. "Come on over here," he directed at Bob, who obliged.

"Looks like you're leavin' us," Hickok greeted.

"Yessir, that would be the case."

"Hell, I was countin' on takin' back what you took from me last evening, sir," Hickok said with a sardonic grin.

Bob replied, "Well, I believe it was the others I won against, mostly. As I remember, you were doing quite handily yourself, sir."

"Well, yes, I guess I do have a reputation to keep up."

From across the room, a shout came from the same poker table where the game took place the night before, "Hickok! Stop jawin' and get your ass over here!"

Hickok shot back with, "You're in my damned seat there, Charlie! Get outta my chair and I'll accommodate'ya."

"No, sir. It's my chair now. We'll see how lucky you be sittin' across from it," came the challenge.

Hickok gave Charlie a humorous finger-salute and turned back to Bob. "That's Charlie Rich over there. He's always after sittin' in my chair. Thinks it's charmed because I win so much. I keep tellin' him it's the cards. It's always the cards, wouldn't you agree, sir?"

Bob nodded, "Yessir, I would agree with that."

"What I don't tell'im is that I sit in that chair with my back to the wall, so's I can keep an eye on who's comin' through the front and back doors... You never know who you might've offended at one time or 'nother," he added as he squinted directly into Bob's eyes.

Bob had noticed that Hickok seemed to have squinted at what he was looking at the night before. He'd thought at the time that the gambler was just concentrating, or, as a seasoned gambler was want to do, playing possum to throw off the others who might be looking for a *tell*... But, now, he could see that Hickok might, indeed, have something wrong with his eyesight and that was what Miss Marchbanks' odd comment meant.

"Nossir, you never know," Bob replied evenly.

"Join me in one last toast then?"

"A toast to what, sir?"

Hickok eased his wide-brimmed hat back on his head of shoulder-length hair. "A toast to good gamblin', good drinkin', good women and a warm place to shit. That good enough, sir?"

"Those would be good enough reasons, sir."

Hickok called to the bartender for two whiskeys. "So..."

Bob leaned his Winchester against the side of the bar and set his saddlebags on the bar top.

Hickok continued with his thought. "...So, what is it you go by again?"

Bob didn't hesitate to answer as the whiskeys were set in front of them. "Oh, nothing special. The name's Robert Duncan from down Fort Randall way.

"Oh, yes, I asked you last night. Gettin' a bit forgetful lately. I know it well. Terrible cook there. Ornery old dough puncher, name of Jasper Spence. He could make a saddle out of a good side of beef. But, he did have a good turn of the cards, I will say that in his favor."

"Grew up nearby on my mother's homestead."

"And, now you're a gambler," Hickok stated as he took down a slug of whiskey.

"Nossir, not at all. I write stories about the Wild West for publications back East."

Hickok reacted with surprise. "Well, I'll be hogtied and branded! I thought for sure you were a professional gambler there, Mister Duncan."

"I do get lucky from time to time."

"Well, then we'll toast to the Wild West writer who gets lucky from time to time." Hickok clicked his glass to Bob's and downed the rest of his drink.

Charlie Rich shouted from the poker table, "Hey, Bill, for crissakes! You're holdin' up the game!"

"Sumbitch can't wait for me to clean'im out," Hickok chuckled. "Sure you won't join us?"

Bob checked his gold pocket watch. "Nossir, it's headin' far past midday and this already bein' the second day of August, I better be headin' out while I've still got light. But I do appreciate the offer, sir."

"Some other time then," Hickok said. Adding good-naturedly, "Maybe, you can write about me and make me famous."

Bob nodded with a slight smile at the jest, "I believe you're already quite famous as it is, Mister Hickok."

Hickok stuck out his hand. Bob took it. "Nice meetin'ya, Mister Duncan."

"Nice meetin' you, Mister Hickok."

Hickok didn't let go of Bob's hand just yet. "How're you with that Peacemaker you're carryin' there?" Hickok asked with a noticeable squint.

"Well, I guess you could say I'm still here."

Hickok kept a firm grasp on Bob's hand. "I prefer my ivory handled Colt 1851 Navy .36 caliber myself. I have two of those beauties that I use in a two-handed cross-draw. Maybe, you and I could get us up a shootin' contest upon your return. Winner takes all. How does that sound, sir?"

Bob let his hand slip out of Hickok's grip. "I believe the odds would be stacked unfairly in your favor, sir."

Hickok grinned at the recognition. "I believe my

reputation might have caught up with me, I'm afraid. Well, good luck to you, Mister Duncan. I look forward to reading one of your stories."

"Thank you, sir."

With that, James Butler 'Wild Bill' Hickok headed over to the empty chair and sat down with his back to the front and back doors.

The main street was alive with activity as Bob stepped into a dry goods general store and purchased a jar of Dr. Peabody's Toothpaste, a new bristle toothbrush, a couple of Eberhard Faber pencils with attached erasers, and a new model lead pencil with a round core called a Joseph Dixon. Bob figured he would try it out when he made his next entry notes into the leather-wrapped notebook he always carried with him. Some dried beans and a wrapped package of smoked meat filled out his order. It would be a ride of several days ahead of him with no towns or stores between Deadwood and wherever he would end up. Although, he did start to formulate a plan of sorts.

At the livery, Bob gave the livery boy four bits extra and saddled up. "Thank you for the advice on where to stay," Bob acknowledged and headed out of the barn.

There were two ways out of Deadwood. It didn't matter which one to Bob, so he headed due north toward the Meade and Belle Fourche areas. Then, if the plan he was formulating in his head came to fruition, he might circle back south and stop in to check on his mother, Millie Mae, if he made it as far as Fort Randall. However, that would depend on what opportunities presented themselves along the way. After all, his efforts were mostly for her behalf as much as they were for his own. Since he could not budge her off of her homestead, to set up in a more comfortable town setting, he had promised himself that he would see to it that his mother had the wherewithal to build a proper house on her property and some sheds and a suitable barn if that's what she wanted. He wasn't there yet, but he had squirreled enough spoils of his trade away in different places to at least give his promise a good start. He had already purchased an expensive iron potbellied stove and stovepipe and had it shipped by stagecoach to the depot at Fort Randall, with instructions to Master Sergeant Bartholomew to help his mother install it in the main room of her sod house.

Once again, he slowed in front of the Gem Theater being constructed and entertained a quick thought of Grace Doyle before heading on down the street.

At midpoint on Main Street, he had to pull up so as not to run into a man who was obviously well into his liquor as he weaved in front of his horse. Bob immediately saw that it was the gambler from the night before that Hickok had introduced as Jack "Broken Nose" McCall. Bob deduced that McCall was quite drunk and, by the dark expression on his face, was still angry as he stepped up onto the boardwalk and headed unsteadily in the direction of the Nuttal & Mann's Saloon.

Bob eased his horse into an easy lope toward the edge of town then reined up short at the sound of a gunshot that rang out back in the direction of Nuttal &

Mann's. Of course, hearing a gunshot in Deadwood was so routine in nature that Bob paid it no mind and clucked his horse forward without looking back.

As he left Deadwood behind, Bob could not get the idea out of his head that a woman had not only held up a stage, but also had gone to the hotel and fleeced a bunch of seasoned poker players as well. And, as far as he could tell, she had done all this alone and was not partnered up with anyone. At least, no one had said as much.

The road north was well worn, with the constant stream of horse mounted travelers, stagecoaches and lumbering oxen teams, pulling covered prairie schooners loaded with adventurous families and their precious possessions; crisscrossing the territory to establish themselves anywhere else but from where they had come from.

Not particularly interested in meeting up with anybody, and sticking to his rule of traveling alone as much as he could, Bob reined his horse off onto a narrow wheel-rutted lane that lead away from the main trail and didn't seem as heavily traveled.

The cottonwoods became denser as he left Deadwood in the distance and, after passing a few last outbuildings, he was quite alone. Alone, until he saw something up ahead.

Bob pulled up on his horse to get a better look, then eased the roan forward. As he got closer, he saw an empty buckboard and horse stopped by the edge of the trees. The horse was still hitched up to the rig, but the driver didn't seem to be around. Probably, relieving himself, he thought and decided to just ride on by and leave it be. Holding up a single driver of a buckboard was not something that interested Bob. His successes came about from not being tempted by greed.

As Bob eased his horse past the rig, he noticed that it seemed familiar. He also saw that the horse hitched to it had a lamed up right front foot that it was tenderly tapping on the ground.

Just after the first rows of cottonwoods, Bob saw something or someone move. "Hello?" he said, as he rested his right hand on his holstered Colt Peacemaker just as a precaution. These were dangerous parts and there was nothing worse than coming upon a hungry desperado or a renegade to ruin your day.

The form within the trees moved and slowly came forward.

Even with her muddied-up white dress, she was a vision to Bob. She stood there not saying a word. Just staring at him. The mud on her dress had already started to dry in the warm sun. However, he could see that the tearstains that ran down her cheeks were fresh and damp.

"You alright?" he offered.

She shook her head, letting her ringlets of shiny auburn hair flutter in the sunlight. Bob felt a certain longing inside. Something he hadn't felt in sometime. Not that he hadn't been satisfied whenever the need arose, because he had. But, this feeling bore a memory of a young girl by the name of Lily Childes with whom he had his first time lay with several years back near Fort Randall. Lily was a *working girl* who had lied about her age to anyone who had asked. Especially to the tough, burly woman and her shady husband who ran the prostitutes near the fort. But, from the first time she and young Bob had laid eyes on each other no questions had to be asked. They had clung to each other whenever the opportunity arose. Lily's bosses knew what was going on, but let it go as long as Lily put in her time with the customers.

It had taken Bob a long time to get over the fact that Lily had suddenly left with a man three times her age and who had more money than Bob could ever imagine having...

"My horse came up lame," the woman answered softly.

Bob eased himself out of his saddle and cinched the reins to the back of the buckboard. "I'll have us a look."

With that, Bob walked slowly up beside the wagon's horse, dragging his hand lightly along the horse's side and up along its neck to ease the animal's anxiety. He could see that the horse's eyes were wide with anticipation. He stroked the side of its head and let it sniff his hand with its large nostrils. Bob saw that the horse was favoring its right front foot. Each time it touched the ground with its hoof, its head immediately started to bob up and down, indicating that it was painful.

"Easy," Bob whispered and slowly reached down and patted its foreleg just above the hoof to get the horse to let him have a look. "Easy girl," Bob murmured as he gained the horse's trust and examined the underside of the hoof. After a moment, he slowly let the foreleg go, rose up, walked over to his saddlebag, and took out a small hoof knife.

"Picked up a stone."

The woman uttered, "Will she be..."

"Sure thing, ma'am, I'll get it out and you can be on your way." With that, Bob went about getting the horse to work with him again and extracted the stone from its hoof. The horse gingerly tried it out and seemed satisfied that it was safe to put some weight on it. Bob took the horse's head by the bit and led it forward a few feet.

"Looks fine now, ma'am." He went back to his saddlebag and dropped the knife into it, then turned to the woman.

"Thank you," she uttered with some noticeable distress in her voice and a failed attempt at a smile.

"Is there anything else I might help with?" Bob asked. He wasn't going to just ride away with her standing there and *Lily* on his mind. That feeling was not passing. It was growing stronger. He walked a few steps closer to the young woman. He could see that there were fresh tears welling up in her eyes and that there was a reddening on her cheek where O'Banyon had smacked her and then sent her flying off the boardwalk into the muck.

"Could I pay you?" she asked.

"No-no, ma'am... but you could tell me your name, if it's all the same."

She hesitated a moment. Her eyelashes fluttered as her face flushed crimson and nearly matched the reddening mark on her cheek.

"Miriam," she answered and stared right into Bob's blue eyes.

"You're the sheriff's wife who I saw back at..."

"Yes!" she interrupted rather curtly.

"Are you alright, then? I mean, after what I saw?"

Miriam didn't answer. She stood there a moment more, then took a step closer to Bob. "What's *your* name?"

Now, the feeling was becoming even more powerful. "Bob Duncan, ma'am."

She stepped up to him and gently touched his cheek. Bob didn't resist. Miriam slid her hand down his arm and cupped his hand into hers without taking her eyes from his. She turned and led Bob back among the cottonwoods until they came upon a small grassy clearing. Without another word, Miriam quietly unbuttoned all of the buttons that were needed to expose Bob's chest. Then she quietly unlaced all the trusses that bound her dress to her.

Lily stood before him again. Lily pressed her firm white breasts into his chest. *Lily* breathed her warm breath into his ear, as she continued to unbutton any buttons that held him in. She had the scent of fresh lilac. A scent not unfamiliar to Bob, as he remembered *Lily* and the magic she had often bestowed upon him.

The sun overhead was approaching late afternoon. "Will I ever see you again?" Miriam asked quietly, as Bob helped her up onto her buckboard.

"Possibly, if I get back to these parts."

"I would like that."

"I would like that as well," Bob replied, then asked, "How will I let you know?"

"Oh, I'll know if you show in Deadwood, but

we'll have to meet here and only here. You should not go any further on this roadway. It leads directly to where I live."

Bob knew what she meant. Meeting up with O'Banyon would be unhealthy for both of them.

As Miriam guided her buckboard on down the narrow roadway, Bob watched as she looked back at him, not once but three times before she disappeared around the bend.

He stood beside his horse a moment more. This had been a new occurrence for him. Something that he had only experienced with *Lily*.

Before he mounted up, Bob reached into a saddlebag and withdrew a small package of three-for-five-cents *Old Virginia Cheroots* and a small, capped metal cylinder of phosphorus matches. Bob didn't smoke much. Cheroots were fairly new west of the Mississippi and were hard to come by because of their popularity. But, this was a special occasion. Although, he was fairly sure that meeting up again with Miriam O'Banyon was not a sure draw to an ace, he hoped that it might be a luck of the draw that they might...

Bob took Miriam's advice and doubled back to the main road. He'd decided to head in the direction of a place known as Scooptown near Belle Fourche. When inquiring about the woman bandit at the Deadwood Wells Fargo Office, Bob had scanned the daily arrival and departing schedules of the northbound stages. There were two a day. One in the morning and one at midday. He would ride until dusk and make camp near the best place along the route to relieve the early morning stage of its spoils.

The stars that night were extra bright because the moon was nowhere in sight. Having fed and watered the roan, Bob settled for some boiled beans and some of the smoked meat, then topped off his meal with what turned out to be the most mouthwatering plum pudding he had ever eaten.

He'd camped a short distance back from the trail, as was his usual arrangement before carrying out his business. He contemplated eating the nest of quail eggs he'd come upon by the small creek where he had made his camp, but decided they would make a hearty breakfast before the stage rolled in.

Using his saddle as a pillow, Bob stretched out on his waterproof poncho and laid his head back. As he had done many times before, he started connecting the bright stars above into the constellations that his mother and his teacher, Miss Lundergan, had taught him as a youngster, and that he had taught to *Lily* when they had laid out in the wild at night and looked up at the same groups of stars. *Miriam*, he thought. Who was this *Miriam*? Would he ever see her again or was it just a dream... just a dream... *just a dream...*

The loud snort from the roan jarred Bob awake with a start and his Colt Peacemaker instantly pointed at who or whatever might be bringing danger into his camp. There wasn't anyone or anything there. His horse was just waking up with the sunrise and ready to start another day.

Bob made quick use of the quail eggs, then

scratched out his camp, making sure any trace of him would be hard to distinguish from the surrounding area. He deduced that the stage would take about three hours out of Deadwood to reach the bend in the trail where Bob would set up a roadblock of a downed cottonwood. But, he found that it would be a bit tricky this time, because several teams of covered wagons had already passed through and there would surely be more to come. That's why Bob had chosen a spot on a tree shrouded rise where he could look back down the trail with his small brass telescope and spot whatever was coming along. The covered wagons were extremely slow. The stage would easily pass them by. Once the stage was at a distance ahead of the prairie schooners, he would skedaddle back, haul the tree across the trail, and wait just out of sight.

Bob heard the approaching stage. He pressed on the black actor's mustache glued to his upper lip and adjusted the green sunglasses covering his blue eyes. He had dressed exactly as he had several days before, so as to let the law in the area get the same description of the same bandit that was operating in the territory. A bandit that did not exist. His horse, with its white star painted on its forehead, twitched its ears in anticipation. The horse knew what to do. They were ready.

The stage closed in. Bob drew his Winchester '73 out of its scabbard, flicked the finger lever and locked in a bullet. He saw the stage driver suddenly pull up on the reins and the guard riding shotgun jerk back on the wooden handbrake.

Bob jammed his short rounded spurs into the

roan. The horse leaped out from the cottonwoods and wheeled around in front of the skidding stage, rearing up on its hind legs, its front hooves pawing frantically at the air. All the while, with Bob aiming his Winchester in the direction of stage drivers. The startled four-horse team thrashed around and tried to wrench free and kick over the traces. As the roan settled back down, Bob leveled his Winchester right at the driver who raised his hands without protest. This stretch of trail had been hit many times before. The guard made not a move toward his gun. They were used to it.

"You're too late, mister."

Bob didn't say anything. He signaled toward the passengers with the barrel of his rifle for them to disembark. "We were hit about an hour back. Took most anything of value. Nothin' left but the clothes on their backs."

The passengers, two men, two women and a young girl, peered fearfully out of the stage opened windows. Not saying a word.

Bob watched both of the drivers closely as he backed his horse to where he could get a better look at the luggage boot at the rear of the stage. The luggage was gone. So was the usual strongbox that would have been stashed under the driver's seat. The top of the stage was cleaned off as well.

"Can we go?" asked the lead driver. "S'nothin' left of value to you. Not even a pocket watch."

Bob felt his blood boiling inside of him. He gritted back any words he felt like blurting out.

Back along the trail, Bob heard the crack of a whip of an approaching team of oxen. Bob backed his horse away from the stage, leaving room for the stage to circle out around the roadblock.

The driver reined the team around the felled tree and back onto the trail. As he passed Bob he said, "T'was a woman."

Bob just sat in his saddle and stared at the driver through his green Civil War sharpshooter sunglasses. "Probably, same's the one what hit the line the other day back before Deadwood."

Bob didn't move or lower his rifle as the driver gave him a slight nod and slapped the long reins over the team's backs and drove the stage on down the trail.

The distant crack of the whip said that the oxen team and its haul were getting closer. Bob and the roan took their leave.

"Fuck!" Bob shouted aloud for the first time in a long time, as he maneuvered his horse among the cottonwoods back to where he would again change into his usual clothing, wrap up the mustache and wash the white greasepaint from the roan's forehead.

Not one to curse much at all, being that his mother raised him on the teachings of the Gospel; Bob just could not hold his anger and frustration in any longer, "Goddammit!" he blasphemed.

BOUDINE

THREE

....And, a mighty, mighty she, she would be...

--

Scooptown was a place where a ragtag town had sprouted along the stage route heading north to the Belle Fourche area of the South Dakota Territory; where families and others had pretty much come to the end of their rope and provisions and wanted to just stop and settle somewhere. Sometimes anywhere would do. It wasn't the official name, but was used in place of what was rumored to soon be given the name of Sturgis, South Dakota, after the Civil War General Samuel D. Sturgis. The men who had hired on to build a new U.S. Army Military Post, that would eventually be called Fort Meade after General George Meade, called it *Scooptown* because that's where they scooped up their wages while working on the fort. Also, the fact that word had spread so rapidly that gold and quick riches had been discovered in the Black Hills was not lost on the Scooptown region, where the spillover from Deadwood had reached.

Scooptown was much smaller and less settled than Deadwood. The law was pretty much nonexistent, allowing the lawless to be as lawless as they desired. Gambling, prostitution and drinking were the prime entertainment and gunfire was a near day and night occurrence.

For Bob, this would be a short stay. Confronting an angry gunslinger was not what he had in mind. He soon found a livery on the main street and paid to have his horse and tack boarded for the night. Then went in search of a room, a bath, a meal, and if possible, a card game to refill his lack of being able to replenish his financial well-being on the trail. *"Goddammit!"* he repeated in his head as he continued to simmer over having his livelihood assaulted by this *woman bandit!* He vowed that if he ever caught up with her, she would receive the brunt of his fury and be run out of the territory for good. Actually, he'd imagined that her head was a large watermelon and that he'd used a blunderbuss on it as target practice, blasting it to smithereens.

Bob deposited his saddlebags on the floor next to the small washstand in the nearly naked-of-furniture room that he found above one of the only saloons that wasn't a converted tent and had actually been completed as a two-story hotel, gambling hall and brothel. The bath he had hoped for would have to wait until the next creek he came upon. As he stripped to his waist and began to wash-up at the washstand, there was a knock at the door. Bob took his Colt Peacemaker from its holster that he'd slung over the bedpost and asked, "Who's there?"

"Me," came a rather gruff female voice.

Bob carefully unlocked and opened the bedroom door a crack, holding his Colt pistol at the ready. He was met by, what he immediately determined from her dress and authoritative demeanor, the madam of the brothel.

"Ma'am?" he questioned.

The burly madam stepped aside and eased forward a rather young woman who she held firmly by her bare arm. The young prostitute smiled demurely up at Bob. He could see that she wasn't at all displeased at the prospect of Bob being a customer. Bob looked at her and, because he was near exhausted and still furious inside, sighed and said with a sense of relief, "Why not."

The meal he finished at the saloon bar was adequate at best. Sowbelly, sourdough, and some sort of greasy fried greens. Bob deduced that the cook wasn't far from a cattle drive chuck wagon and was still working from his chuck box. Fair enough to say that he certainly couldn't hold a candle to the cooking of Lucretia Marchbanks back in Deadwood. But, it would have to make do.

He quietly nursed a whiskey. The good one. He had pushed back the watered-down glass of varnish that was first served up to him, along with a quiet stare that cautioned the bartender that it would be much healthier for him to replace the glass of diluted liquor without any argument. Bob studied the several card games in progress around the smoke-filled, medium-sized saloon. The customary piano player was hunched over the ivories doing his bit. The usual painted ladies were dutifully going about their business. He did get a more than appreciative look from his first acquaintance in Scooptown, as she made her way past him on the arm of a new customer as they headed up the stairs near the end of the long bar. At least, he had that to remember from Scooptown, if not the food. She was by no means Lily

Childes or Miriam O'Banyon, but she had been unexpectedly and appreciatively above average for a working girl. He tried to remember her name... *Ivy*, he thought. Maybe, he would see her again. Maybe not. It didn't matter.

A break in a card game came as a depleted poker player tossed in his last hand for the evening and relinquished his place at a table. Bob hastened over and replaced him.

"You new around these parts?" came the question from the gambler who now held the deal.

Bob didn't answer immediately. He never did. Then, he smiled a bit. "Isn't everyone?" came his good-humored response. Bob's attitude immediately broke the ice and the game began. As Bob anted in, the gambler next to him uttered, "Too bad about ol' Wild Bill."

Bob's interest was piqued, but he just studied his cards without saying anything.

"What about'im?" came a response from across the table.

"Got bushwhacked 't'other day in Deadwood over at Nuttal & Mann's."

"You're kiddin'!" the dealer added.

"Nope, I ain't. Drunken poker player name of Jack McCall came right up behind him and shot him dead right through the back of his head."

That was the gunshot, Bob remembered, as he rode out of Deadwood.

"Damn," another gambler uttered to himself. "Never thought the day would come that Wild Bill Hickok would let someone get the drop on'im." The rest of the table nodded and muttered in agreement. Bob remained silent. He signaled for just one card and the dealer issued such.

"Newspaper dropped off over 't'the stage office said he was holdin' aces and eights. Called it the 'Dead Man's Hand'."

Bob did not let on any interest. He just played out the hand and pulled in the winnings. Something that he imagined Wild Bill Hickok would have done had the situation been reversed.

The game continued for several more hands pretty much in silence. There probably wasn't anyone anywhere who hadn't been swept up in the tall tales that spread through the frontier towns and dime novels about the exploits of one Wild Bill Hickok. Bob included. But, to have actually heard the shot ring out, that was something that not a gambler at the table could say they had heard, except for Bob.

Two of the players folded their hands and quit the game. Bob was feeling ready to do the same himself, although he was not on any kind of time schedule. Maybe a hand or two more. He had played quite well. Not well enough to make anyone angry or accuse him of dealing from the bottom of the deck or palming a card, but well enough to salt away a tidy profit for the night.

As the deal passed over to Bob, a rather slight man dressed in an ill-fitting black suit jacket and pants tucked into black boots, sat in on the game. His black hat was pulled down nearly over his eyes so as not to let anyone get a good look at his face in the dimly lit saloon. Bob dealt the cards to the remaining players. He took two cards. Two other players took two each. The new gambler stayed with what he'd been dealt. Bob noticed he played with his black gloves on. *Odd,* he thought.

The new player won his first hand and then his second. Only taking two cards in all. *Something wasn't right*, Bob thought to himself. When the deal passed to the new gambler, Bob noticed something peculiar. Then, curiosity started to gain a hold on him. The man not only kept his face lowered under the brim of his black hat, he never spoke a word, except for a low mumble that could hardly be heard. He watched very carefully and realized that he was counting the cards just the same as Bob was able to do. That's how he was able to draw to the winning hands. But, that wasn't all of it. There was something else... *something...* Then, it hit him like a bolt of lightning! When the man reached for the deck of cards, Bob had noticed that his wrist between his coat sleeve and glove was nearly hairless and, on closer look, the man appeared not to have a beard. *A woman!* Seemed to shout inside Bob's head. *He's a woman!*

"How many?" The impatient question came from the man next to Bob now dealing the hands.

Bob realized that he was sitting directly across from the woman bandit who had beaten him out of his stagecoach attempts. Not once, but twice!

"How many cards?" came the annoyed voice of the dealer.

Bob heard the question directed at him and looked at his cards. He almost couldn't see them, he was so flushed with anger. His head was swimming. In fact, he nearly destroyed a straight flush by almost arbitrarily giving away two cards. But, he quickly recovered and won the game with what he was holding.

"That's it, gentlemen," Bob uttered politely and shoved his chair back. It was late and Bob was either going to grab the little skunk out of her chair and choke the living shit out of her right then and there, or ease away over to the bar for a whiskey and wait to see where this little clump of horse crap lit off to. *A calm man is an alert man in a bad situation,* his mother had lectured him with when, as a youngster, he had lost a schoolyard fight with an older boy who had laughed after he'd sent Bob home with a bloody nose. Her advice had worked. The bully had never teased or fought with Bob again, after receiving a humiliating thrashing that he would not soon forget.

It wasn't long before Bob's patience was rewarded. The woman bandit quit the game and headed for the stairs to the second floor rooms. Bob deduced that she had paid the premium to acquire a room with *his* proceeds from the robberies, which infuriated him even more. However, he knew that causing a ruckus right out in the open would only lead to trouble for both of them. So, he nonchalantly finished his whiskey and just as casually followed her up the stairs down the hallway to the rooms. After all, she had no idea who he was. Bob had the advantage.

She started to turn the corner a few yards ahead, as Bob arrived at his room door and feigned retrieving his key. She disappeared around the corner. Bob instantly hurried as quietly as possible along the hallway and stopped just short of the corner. He peered around and saw the woman inserting the key into the door. She turned it. Bob tensed. She opened the door and started inside. Bob drew his Colt Peacemaker and leaped into the hallway. In two bounds, he was at the door and behind her. He shoved her in and down hard on the narrow bed in the middle of the small room. He was right on top of her with the muzzle of his gun in her face and cocked, ready to send a lead slug straight into her brain if necessary.

The shove and fall onto the bed had sent her black wide-brimmed hat flying. *Jesus! She has a man's haircut!* For a split second, he thought she actually might be a man after all and he'd made a terrible mistake. That is until she spoke. "What kept'ya?" she asked almost indifferent to her situation.

Her reaction took Bob completely off guard. "Excuse me?" he said. She actually had a mocking grin on her face. "Jesus," Bob uttered under his breath.

"Not hardly. Now are you going to remove that pistol from my face or do I have to resort to..." She stopped.

"To what, you little shit!"

"To this!" Having situated her hand just between Bob's crotch, as they plummeted onto the bed, she suddenly squeezed her hand firmly around his valuables. "If you don't move that Colt away and get off'a me, I'm gonna rip your oysters right out by the roots and feed'em to the house rats and don't think I can't, because I can." She gripped him harder. Her dark almost black eyes told Bob she meant business. He carefully moved the barrel of his Peacemaker away from her face and released the hammer.

"That's better... Now get the hell off'a me. You want to lay on me, you're going to have to strip off your clothes first."

This was not what Bob had expected. He slowly stood up, but kept his Colt drawn. She stood, squared herself before him, and stuck out her hand. "The name's Sally Mae Boudine."

Bob could not believe what was happening. He uttered, as he cautiously shook her hand, "The name's Bob..." She interrupted, "I already know who you are. You be the Bandit Bob Slye that the law is lookin' for aroun' these parts." As she matter-of-factly said this to Bob, she was also relieving herself of her coat, unbuttoning her black shirt and tossing it onto the chair set next to the wall. Bare-chested, she sat on the edge of the bed and lifted a booted foot at Bob. "Pull'em off," she commanded.

Bob was completely baffled, but tried not to show it. He tentatively holstered his gun and pulled off each of her black boots. She then stood up, unbuckled her belt, and let her pants fall to the floor. Bob felt his throat suddenly go dust storm dry. There was his archenemy standing right there a foot away. Stark naked. She was all of five foot and all woman. Even with her man's haircut.

Bob stuttered a bit with, "How... how did you know who I..."

"Get your damned clothes off and lay me down, Slye!" she demanded. Bob could do nothing else but oblige.

FOUR

Back in the day, there was not a soul around,
who could steal a pound from the Bandit Bob Slye.
But, one fateful day, he met up with the beautiful
Sally Mae.
Who looked him right in the eye...and said,
"The name's Sally Mae Boudine. What's yours?"

The panicked wild-eyed steer, trapped skin to wood in the narrow chute, writhed with every muscle and sinew trying to escape. The helpless animal twisted its head around in vain to see what was coming. But, its struggle was all for naught as young Bob Duncan straddled the walkway above the wooden chute and drove the killing spear right into the back of its neck, severing its spinal cord. The animal crashed to the ground with a horrible moan and, still violently twitching, was hauled off with a horse-drawn block-and-tackle. Again and again, Bob stabbed the spear into steer after steer until they turned into a blur of a bellowing, bawling, moaning herd heading toward their demise... The stench of death hung in the air everywhere... Suddenly, the penned in herds of cattle massed and started battering down the acres of cattle yard corrals; escaping and blindly stampeding toward Bob...

He awoke with a start and sat straight up in bed. Where was he? He was in his room in Scooptown above the saloon. His room. Not her room. He started to turn out of bed and felt the tingling pain coming from his back. When he stood, he felt as if he'd hit the pummel of his saddle between his legs. He was naked as a jaybird. Every muscle in his body felt stiff and sore. As he stood in front of the mirror over the washbasin, he turned to see what was causing the stinging on his back. Long red scratch marks. Then he remembered. She was like nothing he had ever experienced. Nothing less than a wildcat! He examined the red bite marks on his neck and wondered if anyone else would notice them.

The door opened. He hadn't locked it. In fact he didn't remember leaving her room during the night. Sally Mae Boudine stood in the doorway fully dressed in her black gambler's duds. Grinning at him. "Y'all look like you've been in a fight there, Slye."

"Don't ever call me that!" he shot back.

"Oh, that's right. You're not who you say you are," she answered, cocking her head. "Anyways, we got some talkin' to do. There's a small cook shack near t'other end of town. Serves ox-piss coffee and a pretty good flapjack that'll stick to your ribs. Meet me there," she ordered and turned to leave, then added, "and don't forget your mustache."

Bob stared incredulously at the empty doorway, then back at his reflection in the mirror. His hand absently touched the bite marks on his neck.

The cook shack probably had not been there for very long, but already looked rundown and seedy. Just another frontier venture that was sure to go bust in very short order. Bob entered through the door of the board-fronted tent and walked over to the bench-table where Sally Mae Boudine was seated reading a day old newspaper and drinking a tin cup of coffee. Bob sat. The unshaven mustached cook came over and set a tin cup of coffee in front of him. "What'll it be then?" he drawled without emotion or any hint of humanity.

Bob started to answer, "Ah..."

Boudine spoke over him, "Two orders of flapjacks and fried eggs."

The cook lugged away and disappeared through the flap entrance in the back of the six bench-table tent.

Bob breathed in deeply, trying to remain calm. Boudine set the newspaper down on the table and tapped it with her gloved finger. The headline read: DEAD MAN'S HAND – ACES and EIGHTS! She tapped the etched picture of Wild Bill Hickok and said, "His eyes were goin' and he was dead broke. Owed damned near everythin' he had."

Bob nodded, she went on, "I drew down on'im. Calamity Jane, too." Bob looked at her skeptically. "I was in Buffalo Bill Cody's travelin' Wild West Show for a bit. They had this quick draw act whereby they drew down on me. I was supposed to lose." Her quirky grin showed Bob there was more to the story.

"What happened?" he asked.

"Ha! I kept winnin', that's what happened. So, they told me to be on my way. Also, because they couldn't stand the fact that a woman who looked like a sixteen year old boy could out draw them and shoot the eye out of a fly at fifty paces." She shrugged.

Bob was getting more irritated by the minute and

eased the newspaper off the table onto the wood plank floor. He leaned forward and, in a hushed but firm voice, asked, "How the hell did you know about the mustache?"

She leaned right into him, "Same ways I learned your name of Slye."

They both sat there almost nose to nose. Not saying a word. The cook lugged up to the table and set down two tin plates of flapjacks and eggs. "More coffee?" he muttered. Bob waved him off. He hadn't touched his. Boudine indicated she would. The cook went off to get the pot. Bob sat back, staring right at Boudine.

"Look," she said, setting her cockiness aside, "I followed you. Saw you put on the mustache and paint that white spot on your horse. You looked just like them wanted posters they'd nailed up."

"Why were you following me?" he demanded.

She leaned in, "Because the three times 'afore that, you beat me to it and I wasn't gonna let that pass without seein' who was gettin' the better of me."

Bob just stared at her for a moment. She sat back and stared right back at him. "Now, you know how it feels," she uttered softly.

Bob finally took a sip of coffee and instantly spit it on the floor. "Told'ja," Boudine laughed, "Ain't Arbuckle's Ariosa, that's f'sure." She then started digging into her flapjacks and eggs. "Worked up a terrible hunger since last night," she chuckled with her mouth full. Bob noticed that, from time to time, she sniffed and would wipe her nose on her sleeve.

Outside on the board walkway in front of the cook shack, the two stood quietly until there was no one in earshot. "So, are we agreed, then?" Boudine offered.

Bob hesitated, then answered, "'Fraid so."

Boudine offered her hand. "Shake on it," she demanded. Bob shook her hand. Boudine pulled down on the brim of her hat and said, "I'll leave town first. Head due north. We'll meet up and formulate a plan." She turned and headed up the boardwalk in the direction of the livery. Bob stood there and watched her go, then noticed another newspaper, *The Black Hills Pioneer*, on the bench outside the cook shack. He picked it up, sat on the bench and read the story about the murder of Wild Bill Hickok.

FIVE

The sparks flew between the two...
They stuck together like horse-hooves glue...

The trail to Belle Fourche was not as well traveled as the ones heading in and out of Deadwood. Mostly used by those who might have tried searching for gold for a bit, but realized all too soon that it was a very precarious and extremely dangerous business. And, therefore, turned their attentions toward the fertile and abundant Belle Fourche rivers and lands; especially the farmers who thought that growing crops and livestock to supply the fur traders and gold and silver miners would be a much better suited enterprise for themselves and their families.

Bob had waited about an hour before riding out of Scooptown. He didn't know just where or when he would meet up with Sally Mae Boudine, but he knew for sure that he would. Boudine had hatched a plan for them to join forces and split their new venture right down the middle. "Fifty-fifty," they'd agreed upon.

It was well past high noon when they finally met up. Bob had come upon a small river and found a place off the beaten path to water his roan and strip down to finally take that bath he'd hoped for. As he stood waist deep and lathered up with a bar of goat's milk soap, he suddenly heard something coming at him from behind. He whirled around just as a bare-naked Sally Mae Boudine made a running dive from the riverbank and splashed under the water right next to him. He was stunned. She didn't surface immediately. Bob looked around. She still didn't surface. Then he felt the firm tug on his privates and jumped back as Boudine broke through the surface laughing loudly at her joke. "Caught the minnow there, Bob!" she exclaimed in a moment of sheer joy.

"Dammit!" Bob shouted. That didn't stop Boudine from jumping up on his naked body, wrapping her arms tightly around his neck, her legs around his waist and planting a big openmouthed kiss right on his lips.

The rest of the afternoon pretty much followed more of what they both seemed to be hankering for. As they lay side by side on the mossy riverbank, Bob uttered, "If you keep up bitin' and clawin' me, there won't be nothin' left."

"I'll have to keep that in mind," she joshed and rolled over on top of him, starting all over again.

There was a chill in the air that said the season might be in for an early change. Bob built a fire and boiled up some dried beans. Boudine contributed the rabbit she'd shot and skinned. As they ate their meal, it was down to business.

"Anyone else ever found out about the

mustache?" Boudine asked between biting some roasted meat off a rabbit bone.

"No... none that I know of."

She chuckled, "Pretty good plan. Had me fooled for a bit. Where'd you come upon it?"

Bob wasn't so sure he wanted to answer that. "Anyone else know you're a girl?"

"Woman."

"A woman then. Anyone else know?"

Boudine flipped the finished rabbit bone into the fire. "Can't say as I know. Don't think so."

Bob looked at her for a moment, then said, "Well, they do in Deadwood and the stage driver told me as much."

"That right?"

Bob sipped some coffee from his tin cup. "That's right and the stage driver outside of Scooptown said so as well."

"What're you sayin' then?" Boudine asked with a sense of suspicion.

"What I'm sayin' is that more'n me know about you not bein' a man than you think."

"Is that right... So what?" she said back to him.

"Well, it means that everyone's going to be on the lookout for a woman bandit, so we better do a little better about seein' that they don't."

This surprised Boudine a bit. There was a sense of relief in her voice. "You got any ideas about that then?"

"Might. I'll be thinkin' on it."

She paused for a moment and stared into the flickering fire. Then she asked, "You didn't answer my question."

"What question?"

"About the mustache. Where'd you come upon it."

Bob paused before answering. "Why do you need to know?"

"Because if I'm going to be in cahoots with someone, I like to know about'em."

Bob sighed, then, "A while back, I met up with this travelin' Irish singer who was workin' in a tent saloon in Deadwood... T'were some time ago... She gave it to me."

"Boudine cocked her head to the side a bit, looking at Bob, and then asked, "A woman singer?"

"Ah, yes, why?"

"Did'ja lay with her?"

"That's none of your concern." Bob reprimanded.

"Maybe it is, maybe it ain't. I was just wonderin' if she was better'n'me," she challenged.

Bob sighed and shook his head with a little exasperation.

"Well, was she?" Boudine teased.

"Will you stop it!"

She kept it up, as she picked up a small burning stick from the edge of the fire and flicked at him. "Was she?" she demanded.

"Dammit-to-hell, Boudine!" Bob almost shouted as he brushed the sparks off his clothes.

"You can tell me there, Slye."

"I told you never to call me that!"

"I won't if'in you tell me."

"You're crazy, you know that?"

"Just tell me. Was she better'n'me?"

Bob gritted in silence for a moment then answered with, "She was different..."

Boudine didn't answer. Just studied Bob. Then, softly said, "You liked her didn't you?"

Bob just stared into the fire; his mind taken up with the Irish singer Grace Doyle. Boudine broke the silence, "Do you like *me*?"

Bob buried his face in his hands in muffled exasperation, "Oh-my-lord."

Boudine sniffed and inadvertently wiped her nose on her sleeve...

Bob and Boudine slept in separate bedrolls that night. Bob hoped the stampeding cattle wouldn't be showing themselves.

A loud pistol shot brought Bob bolt upright on his bedroll. He ripped his Peacemaker out of its holster. His eyes darted around the campsite, just as a dead cock pheasant arched through the air from the other side of a large bush and landed at his feet with a thump. "Breakfast!" Boudine shouted out.

"So, Mister Bob Duncan, did you think on what I should be doin' so's not to look like a woman?"

Bob rose up from the edge of the riverbank, having finished rinsing out the coffee cup and tin dish. "Yes, I did," he said and headed over to his horse to put them into his saddlebags.

"Well, are you going to tell me or do I have to

guess?" Boudine asked, as she scratched out the campfire with a tree branch.

Bob turned to her. "Did you talk to them when you held'em up?"

She had not expected the question. "Sure as hell did. Let'em know where they'd end up if'n they didn't do as I says."

"That might be where you put a spoke in your wheel."

"I don't understand. D'you mean you don't say nothin'?"

"That's right. Not a word. They don't need me to tell'em what I want'em to do. The Winchester does the talkin'," Bob said. "That way, all they have to go on is what they see. If you talk to them the way you talk to me, they sure as hell're going to know you're different."

Boudine stepped on some smoldering ash and put it out, then asked, "Anythin' else?"

"Do you wear a bandana?"

"No, why?"

"No beard. Your face is as smooth as piglet's ass."

This really started to stick in her craw. "Maybe, I should wear the goddamned mustache then."

Bob pursued, "Show me your arm," he asked.

"What for?" she asked back with a heightened sense of fluster.

"Put your hand out like you're going to shake my hand."

Reluctantly, she extended her hand to him. He waited a moment to see if she noticed anything.

"Look, if you think you're catchin' a weasel asleep

here, you got another..."

"Look at your wrist and arm there," Bob said, indicating where her arm was extended beyond her coat sleeve.

She looked, "What about it? I don't see nothin'.

"No hair. No hair on your arm there. Clean as a whistle. Looks like a woman's arm to me."

Boudine noticeably flushed with the evidence presented to her. Bob turned to his saddlebags and closed them up. He then felt under his horse's belly, checked the cinch, and pulled up on it.

"Do I get to ask you a question then, Mister Bob Duncan?" came from behind him. He turned and shrugged to Boudine, who he could see was noticeably chagrinned.

"Where's your bits and pieces?"

"What?" he answered quizzically.

"Where do you stow all the loot you get from your holdups?"

"What's it your business for?"

"Well, if'n we're supposed to be fifty-fifty partners I should know where you keep all your swag, don't'cha think?"

"Where do you keep yours?" Bob came back with.

"Nossir. My question. You first," she fired back.

Bob hesitated, then, "Here and there."

She stifled a laugh. "Here'n'there? Are you joshin' me? Here'n'there?" Bob started to comment further, but she held up her hand and said, "How do you know where it all is then?"

Bob turned and opened a saddlebag and took out

his leather-wrapped notebook. "It's all in here."

She was incredulous, "In there? You keep it all in there?"

"That's right. I know where everything is. It's all hidden real good."

Boudine challenged him, "Can I see that there notebook?"

Bob handed it to her. Boudine flipped through the pencil scribbled notes, then looked at Bob, "This don't make no sense. It's just chicken scratch."

"Makes sense to me."

"Well, then, what if you lose this or it's stolen or somethin'? Tell me that," she demanded as she waved the notebook at him.

Bob tapped the side of his head with his index finger. "It's all in here."

Boudine handed the notebook back. She studied him for a moment then said, "That may be so. I saw the way you were countin' cards t'other night. Almost as good as me. But, what if you're bushwhacked or end up like Wild Bill, what then, huh? All your bits and pieces go to rot. All for nothin'."

Bob wrapped the soft leather around the notebook and put it back into the saddlebag. He didn't answer because he didn't have one.

"Cat's got your tongue on that one, don't it, Mister Bob Duncan." Boudine walked over to her horse, having already saddled it up. She mounted in a smooth jump into the saddle without using the stirrup. "Looks like you and me only just begun talkin' things out." She clucked to her horse and reined it in the direction back to the trail. Bob mounted up and followed, wondering just who the hell this ornery little whippersnapper was and how she ended up traveling with him.

There were clouds beginning to roll in overhead that brought a chill with them. Nothing to worry about, but something to be on the lookout for nonetheless. After riding along in silence for a while and, having passed by an oxen drawn prairie schooner headed toward Belle Fourche with a family aboard, Boudine asked, "What do you expect to do with what you squirreled away?"

"I expect to be able to move my mother off'en that homestead and onto a proper farm with a real house instead of the heap of sod she calls a home. The summers are hellish hot and the winters are as cold as a witch's teat."

"She sounds like a good person," came Boudine's response.

"She..."

Bob didn't get to answer. In a blur, a burly, bearded highwayman burst from the trees along the trail and wheeled his mount in front of them. The Confederate Army rifle he leveled at them both told Bob and Boudine all they needed to know. Bob steadied his horse.

"Get off!" the bandit demanded.

Bob glanced at Boudine. She was focused on the bandit.

"Now!"

Bob eased down from his saddle.

"You there!" the bandit shouted at Boudine. Then, to Bob he demanded, "Hand them reins to me.

Easy. Don't make no moves!" Bob carefully handed his horse's reins up to the bandit who snatched them with his free hand. Bob backed away, keeping his hands raised. The bandit shouted at Boudine, "I said get your ass down! Now!" Boudine nodded and started to dismount, Bob's horse began to nervously back up, pulling on its reins. For a split second, the bandit lowered his rifle. Then, just as quickly brought it up in the direction of Boudine and pulled the trigger. The bullet just missed and splintered a small tree branch just to the right of Boudine's horse. It was all that Boudine needed. In mid-dismount, standing straight up on one foot in the stirrup, she whipped her pistol out of its holster and fanned two quick shots at the bandit, hitting him once in each shoulder. In complete shock, the bandit dropped his rifle and the roan's reins from his useless hands and spit out, "You little fuck! I should'a killed you!" Boudine didn't hesitate as she pulled the trigger again and sent a lead slug ripping right into his skull. Dead on between his eyes.

Bob stood there in complete disbelief as he watched the bandit stiffen wild-eyed, and then topple like a fallen tree onto the ground with a thud.

"Jesus Christ," Bob uttered.

"He had nothin' to do with it," Boudine replied matter-of-factly and reloaded her pistol.

Bob gathered up the reins of his and the dead bandit's horse. He then looked at Boudine, "Why'd you kill'im?"

"It was my King-Queen-Ace shot. That's what I used to do in the Wild West Show. Only them was cards tossed in the air. T'was what made old Wild Bill ornery about me. I never missed. Sometimes he did."

As the dark clouds gathered above, getting more ominous by the minute, Bob started to drag the bandit's dead body off into the bushes.

"Wait," Boudine ordered. She bent over the body, removed the bandit's gunbelt, and holstered revolver. Taking out the pistol, she held it up to Bob. "Well, lookie here! A damned ol' LaMat Grape Shot. Has two barrels. Top one shoots a lead slug and, if'n you choose, the bottom one lets go with a shotgun load. Hell, that would'a hurt some. Haven't seen one of these since I don't know when."

"Anythin' else you want off'n'im?" Bob asked.

"No. He stinks to high heaven."

Bob bent down and started dragging the body off into the bushes beside the trail.

"Varmints'll make short work of that piece of cowshit," Boudine muttered, as she picked up the bandit's rifle.

Bob emerged from the bushes. Boudine held up the rifle. "Nice Sharps Carbine here. He must've been a Reb."

"Makes no matter now." Bob went to the bandit's horse and opened the saddlebags.

"Anythin' useful?" Boudine asked.

Bob took out a good-sized leather pouch and opened it. "Twenty-dollar gold pieces."

"Fifty-fifty!" Boudine reminded him, as she slung the holstered LaMat Revolver over her saddle horn.

"You going to keep that old thing?" Bob asked, as he poked through the saddlebags and looked at the contents.

"Hey, ya'never know when you might want to send a shotgun blast at somethin' or someone," she chuckled.

"They don't make loads for that, you have to mold'em yourself."

"Sometimes you only need one shot and it's presently fully loaded."

Bob shook his head at Boudine's logic and looked up at the sky, as a rumbling came from a distance, "Storm headin' our way."

"Yessir, better be movin' on," Boudine concurred. She handed the bandit's Sharps rifle to Bob who slipped it into the scabbard on the bandit's horse. "What're we going to do with the horse?"

Bob tied the horse's reins to one of the saddle strings and mounted the roan. "Sell it first chance," he said and let out a "chirk" to his horse to start forward along the trail. Boudine followed.

The dark clouds had exploded into a wind-whipped deluge. Bob and Boudine had donned their ponchos and were huddled on their horses under a tree, as sheets of wind-driven rain beat down on them. A large dark shadow emerged from the gray light on the trail. Slowly, it lumbered forward. As it neared Bob and Boudine, it appeared to be the oxen team pulling the covered prairie schooner with the family aboard that they had passed early on. Seeing Bob and Boudine, the man driving the team pulled them to a stop.

"You folks alright?" he shouted over the pelting rain.

"Might ask you the same, sir," Bob shouted back.

"I'm about to pull aside until this lets up. You're welcome to join us and dry off if'n you're of a mind," the man offered.

Bob touched the brim of his *Boss of the Plains* hat and nodded. He then dismounted and, fighting the wind and rain whirling around him, went over to the front of the team of oxen and pulled the yoke in the direction of the sheltering trees.

Inside the covered wagon, the waterproof canvas bonnet flapped hard against the wooden bows that held it in place, but at least it was dry. Bob and Boudine huddled into a space between the wooden boxes, a spinning wheel and canvas wrapped belongings of the family. There was a loud crack of thunder and a bright flash of lightning from outside.

"Nathan Pickering," the man said holding out his hand to Bob and Boudine. "This here's my wife, Abigail; my daughter, Sarah; and that's our youngest, my son, Ben, over under the driver's box with that shivering hound."

Bob shook Nathan's hand. "Bob Duncan. This here's... ah..." He hesitated, realizing he had never introduced Boudine to anyone before and was at a loss as how to do so. Boudine shoved out her hand. "Sally Mae Boudine," she announced without any shilly-shally.

Both Nathan and his family looked quizzically at Boudine for an awkward moment. "Thought I was a man, right?" she said with a smirk at Bob.

"Well, yessir... I mean, ma'am," Pickering answered, "I guess we did at that. I'm sorry if'n..."

"Makes no matter to me. Happens all the time...

don't it, Bob?"

Bob nodded with a bit of a tightness in his jaw.

Boudine whispered to Bob, "Guess I won't be needin' the mustache."

"Where're y'all headed?" Nathan asked.

"Possibly up toward Belle Fourche country," Bob answered.

"Yankton," Boudine interjected.

Bob looked at her. They had never discussed heading to Yankton, which was due southeast and just across the Missouri River. He then added, "It's a possibility that we might head over to Yankton. Not really sure of that as yet." Boudine could see his jaw tensing again. She got a kick out of it.

"Not much for fur trappin' in Belle Fourche," Boudine chimed in and elbowed Bob in his ribs with a grin.

Pickering picked up the conversation, "Well, we're a farmin' family and I hear tell the land around Belle Fourche and the three rivers is ripe for farming. We tried panning and minin' for gold, but it was a fool's folly we quickly found out, so we're off to settle down up there. That's what those bags of seed corn and wheat are for," he said and indicated the sewn cloth bags stacked in the back corner of the wagon.

"That's a good amount of far-thinkin' there, Mister Pickering," Bob said.

Pickering added, "And, Belle Fourche is French for *Beautiful Fork* where the three rivers come together. So, we're hopin' it'll be a good omen for our family. The Good Lord willin'."

Bob nodded. Boudine was quiet.

"Do you read the Bible, Mister Duncan?"

Bob hesitated for a moment, then answered, "I was raised on The Scriptures, sir."

That seemed to satisfy Pickering...

As quickly as the storm had disgorged its torrent, it just as quickly vanished over the horizon. The late afternoon sun poured its rays down through the trees that were bright with the wet sheen of nature's bath.

Bob stood outside the covered wagon with Nathan Pickering and Boudine. Bob held the reins to the dead bandit's horse. "We'd like to pay you for your kindness, sir," Bob said to Nathan.

"Wouldn't have it, sir," Nathan said with a smile. "We were glad for the company and conversation."

"It's already been decided. This here horse and tack we found wanderin' about and there's no sign of a brand on it, and we don't have the will to carry it along. Also, there's a Confederate Sharps Carbine in the scabbard and some extra cartridges in the saddlebags. We're thinkin' it belonged to a Reb highwayman who might've come to a bad end, if you understand what I'm sayin', sir." Bob stared directly into Nathan Pickering's eyes and handed him the reins to the dead bandit's horse without looking away. Nathan apprehensively took the reins and looked over at Boudine. She had the same look in her eyes that Bob had; that told Pickering not to look a gift horse in the mouth and to take it without asking any questions.

"I'm sure you're going to need an extra mount out there on your new farm, and that Sharps rifle shoots real straight in case you run into a renegade band or an ornery varmint," Boudine said.

Nathan nodded and uttered a bit nervously, but nonetheless thankfully, "I do thank you for this gift and we will make good use of it, I can assure you. We wish you both Godspeed in your travels. God bless you both."

Bob touched his fingers to the brim of his hat and mounted up on his roan. Boudine acknowledged Abigail Pickering and did her smooth jump-mount to impress the children.

"We're off then," Bob said to the family and let out a "chirk" that sent his horse into a trot. Boudine nodded to the family and followed, leaving the Pickerings to themselves.

The sunset on the horizon was a bright orange that spread out from afar to right on over their heads.

"Why did you say we were headin' to Yankton?" Bob asked, as they continued along the trail.

"Because, I'll be damned if I'm goin' into the Belle Fourche territory. There ain't nothin' there 'cept some smelly old French fur trappers and a few squalid dirt farmers. Nothin' there for me and I'll bet two aces with one up my sleeve that you won't find nothin' there for yourself."

"Yankton's a far ride from here."

"That's right and they got stages rollin' in and out every day and riverboats right there on the Missouri River and the railroad crosses through goin' west and they got saloons and cook shacks and gamblers just waitin' to be fleeced, or did you forget that's the business we're in."

"I also hear they built a big stockade there."

"That was for the Sioux, not for us. Anyway it was torn down a while back because the Sioux never attacked," Boudine explained.

Bob decided not to pursue the conversation. She'd made her point.

That night, with the rain having cleansed the air, Bob lay on his bedroll by a small fire with his head settled on his saddle and penciled a few notes into his leather-covered notebook. Boudine had wandered off into the woods to take care of her business and wash up in a small running creek nearby. They hadn't spoken all that much on the ride. Just snippets about how they would go about their next enterprise. Nothing that would expose anything personal about either of them. Bob tucked the new Eberhard Faber pencil inside the notebook and wrapped the leather cover around it. As he placed it under his saddle, he heard Boudine coming back from the creek. She was barefoot with only her woven man's shirt unbuttoned and barely covering her. She set the rest of her clothes next to her bedroll that was spread out a few feet from Bob's. Then, without a word, she straddled Bob and reached down and quickly flipped his belt from its buckle and proceeded to pull down his trousers just enough to expose him. She then sat directly down onto him and had her way.

SIX

...The fire they started roared both night and day.
Leveling anyone of a mind to get in their way...

The over three hundred miles of trail from Scooptown to Yankton, South Dakota was not an easy trek, even for the most seasoned traveler. Anything and everything could and usually did happen. The Sioux, and other tribes of indigenous peoples, had plenty of reasons to be angry about the huge influx of gold seekers and settlers who arrived in droves, after the discovery of gold by the expedition of George Armstrong Custer that overwhelmed their lands in a matter of a few years. Legally or illegally, it didn't seem to matter. As in the case of Deadwood, it seems the United States Government turned a blind eye to the Treaty of 1868, that gave the Sioux the lands in and around what became Deadwood, South Dakota.

Yankton was much more built up and settled than most areas of the Dakotas. With its immediate access to the Missouri River as an inland trade route, Yankton was designated the Capital of the Dakota Territory by the President of the United States, James Buchanan, in 1861. It was a hustle and bustle of activity, both reputable and nefarious. It was just a matter of which side one chose, as to how, where and when they carried out their business. With the Bandit Bob Slye and his new partner, Sally Mae Boudine, that demarcation had already been set in stone.

"When we get near to Yankton, let me take the lead," Boudine stated, as the two sat on their mounts and looked back on the barren, narrow area of the Missouri River they had just successfully forded.

"Why is that?"

"Because I've already been here and you ain't. I come here with the Wild West Show and I know the peculiars of this town," Boudine underscored.

Bob indicated that they move forward, "As you say," he muttered.

"By the way, I never asked you. How much did that highwayman's gold pouch add up to?" Boudine asked after Bob.

"Doesn't matter..."

"What the hell it doesn't matter! Fifty-fifty! That means half is mine!" Boudine reiterated.

"I gave it to the family back on the trail," Bob calmly informed her.

Boudine instantly reined up her horse to a dead stop and uttered, flabbergasted, "You did what?"

Bob just kept riding on a few more yards, then stopped and turned his horse in Boudine's direction.

"I don't believe this!" Boudine said, nearly shouting in exasperation. "You give it away to someone you don't even know?"

Bob calmly reached around, opened a saddlebag, lifted out the fist-sized pouch of gold coins, and jingled it at Boudine with a big grin on his face. Then he put it back into the saddlebag.

Boudine's eyes went black with a sudden rage that erupted with the fury of a volcano. "You sumbitch! I'm comin' for-ya!"

Bob made the immediate decision that creating a distance between them was the best choice. He wheeled the roan around in a tight turn and spurred his mount into a dead-on gallop.

Boudine was not about to let this go as just a joke on her. She lunged forward over her saddle horn. Her horse charged into a mad dash after Bob, who could be heard laughing out loud as he raced over the trail with Boudine in hot pursuit. "I'm going to shoot your lyin' ass, Slye! You hear me, Bob Slye! I'm gonna cut off your tail and roast it on a spit!"

Far from carrying out her threats, Boudine and Bob celebrated their having traveled over three hundred treacherous miles to arrive within spitting distance of Yankton, by frantically rolling around on their bedrolls in grand fits until they lie there under the stars exhilarated and completely exhausted.

Bob awoke at first light. He was still naked as a jaybird. So was Boudine curled up next to him. He looked down at her with a pleasant smile on his face and lightly tried to pick off a twig that had entangled itself in her short hair. Immediately, Boudine went for her pistol, slapping her bare hip where the holster would have been, had she been wearing it. "Whoa, girl," Bob hushed. Boudine blinked awake and looked around at their encampment and at their clothes strewn about. "Lucky I'm not a bounty hunter."

Boudine reached an arm up around Bob's neck and pulled him into a ferocious kiss that sent them into an early morning frolic.

"You never told me why you chose to do what you're doin'?" Boudine asked Bob, as they finished a late breakfast of hardtack and jerky, washed down with Arbuckle's.

"If they have a slaughterhouse there in Yankton, I'll show you."

"Well, they do have a hefty cattle yard, as I recall, and a railhead that goes on up there to Des Moines, Iowa, so's I would think there'd be a slaughterhouse about. Did you work in one?"

"I'll show you... What about you?" Bob asked.

"Do you really want to know?" Boudine answered with a sense of seriousness.

"You did say it was going to be fifty-fifty with us," Bob said, as he poured the coffee grounds out of his tin cup onto the campfire.

"The short of it is that I was sick and tired of all them ass-grabbin' cowboys in the Wild West Show tryin' to get into my knickers, and it seemed like an easy way to get what I needed." She didn't elaborate.

"That's all?" Bob asked, a bit doubtfully.

"That's all for now," Boudine answered flatly then abruptly stood up, dumped her coffee grounds onto the fire and headed over to her horse.

Bob watched her for a moment, then stood,

collected his bedroll and saddle and headed over to the roan.

The way into Yankton was an easy ramble compared to the treacherous trek they had achieved. As they approached the outskirts of what had become a bustling center of commerce, because of its access to the Missouri River and a major stop of the new railroad link to the West, the two new partners in banditry exchanged ideas on how best to set out on their new venture...

"You best see a barber; you're startin' to look like a woman."

"Don't go worryin' about me there, Mister Duncan. I've got a few things to see to a'fore we set out on our first business enterprise."

"Do you know of a saloon or a boarding house?"

"Down the far end of the main street there's a two story hotel where we put up last time I was here. It's not a saloon, so's we'll have to go elsewhere to find us a decent card game. But, they do have some painted ladies who use the place, so's I better not see you gettin' funny with any of'em, if you want to keep your johnson from becomin' separated from you."

"I'm not so sure I like the way you're talkin' to me there, Boudine, I'm used to workin' alone."

"Look here, Slye! I like you and I'm damned sure you like me by the way you been actin', so let's not let any hankerin' get in the way."

"We should meet up someplace, after we get the lay of the land, so's we can make a plan."

"We'll go into town separately. There's a livery 'bout

halfway along the street on the right. I'll board my horse and head for the hotel. You hold up for a time, then come on in. Then, I suggest you get a room at the hotel for yourself and strip down and spread yourself out on the bed. I'll find you."

Bob watched Boudine as she headed in the direction of Yankton at a trot. He waited until she disappeared over a rise about a half mile away, then "chirked" the roan forward at an easy walk.

Other than his short time in Wichita, Kansas, Bob had stuck to operating in and around the South Dakota gold rush towns that suddenly sprouted along the trails from Spearfish, Lead, Belle Fourche and Deadwood. They were easier to navigate and harder for any law to circle in on him, as he went about his business...

"Have you ever kilt anyone there, Bob?"
"Nope, can't say as I have."
"You mean no one ever drew down on ya?"
"I didn't say that."
"You mean, anyone who drew on ya backed down?"
"I'm still here."
"Hell, you must be pretty fast on the draw there, Bob Slye Duncan."
"Fast enough."

The closer he got to Yankton, the more he could see that things were much different from Deadwood or Scooptown. The houses and homesteads on the outskirts were mostly wooden structures with proper windows, doors and outhouses. Quite a few had barns, as well as outbuildings. There were a few of the old frontier sod houses, but just a smattering. He even pulled up to a stop to watch children playing outside a properly built schoolhouse. Certainly, a far cry from the one-room soddy where he had learned to read and write; among the other things that Miss Lundergan had taught him. This, indeed, was going to be a new experience for the Bandit Bob Slye.

SEVEN

They scorched the earth beneath their feet.
Fleecing those who couldn't stand the heat...

...The longhorn bore down on him, snorting sprays of red phlegm from its flared nostrils; its mouth and lolling tongue spewing a river of blood and innards, as the panicked animal rammed its wild-eyed head against the narrow wood-planked enclosure. Straddled above the bellowing steer was young Bob Duncan, ramming the killing spear over and over again into the dying animal's upper spine... The longhorn dropped to the ground with a thud, its hooves rapping in death throes against the thick planks. Instantly, it was replaced by another bawling steer... and another... and another...

The rapping noise became louder and louder. Bob sat bolt upright on the bed and ripped his Peacemaker out of its holster lying next to him. Realizing that he was in the hotel room in Yankton and that someone was knocking impatiently on the room door, Bob leapt off the still made up bed and went to the door without opening it. Holding his pistol at the ready, he asked, "Who's there?"

A muffled voice uttered, "Open up."

Bob slowly turned the key in the lock and eased

the door open a bit, still cautiously holding his pistol in case he needed to defend himself. Through the space between the door and the doorjamb, Bob made out the form of a woman in a dark brown, full-buttoned dress and a slatted long bonnet that made it difficult to see who was wearing it.

"What is it you want? I'm not lookin' for a woman at this time, so you best..."

Bob didn't get a chance to finish. The woman in the slatted bonnet suddenly came crashing through the opening, sending Bob nearly toppling onto the floor. As Bob regained his balance and brought his Peacemaker up in the direction of the intruder, the woman stood there in the middle of the room and removed the bonnet and tossed it onto the bed. Her head and face were completely covered with a tightly knotted black scarf with eyeholes cut into it that she reached up and removed.

"Boudine!" Bob uttered, completely befuddled.

It was indeed Boudine, standing there in the buttoned-up dark brown dress. "Ha!" she guffawed with a wide grin and the sparkling eyes of someone who had just performed a great joke on someone she knew. "Lucky I wasn't a bounty hunter there, Slye!" she said, giving him back what he'd said to her just a morning ago.

Bob returned the Peacemaker to its holster. "What're you doin' in that getup?" he said to Boudine.

"What're you doin' still dressed there, Bob? Thought I told'ja to be all naked when I got here," Boudine teased.

Bob sat on the edge of the bed. "Dog tired. Fell asleep."

"Well, we got a lot to talk 'bout. But first, help me outta this goddamned woman's tent," Boudine ordered as she turned her back to Bob. "S'got more buttons than a dog's got fleas, I swear."

Bob started to unbutton the back of the fitted dress, as Boudine hurriedly worked to unbutton the front. He noticed that she was sniffling a bit.

"You got yourself a cold there?"

"No, I ain't. Just the mustard weed," Boudine replied then presented herself fully undressed, standing right in front of Bob. Her eyes were black with anticipation, as she set her hands on his chest and eased him toward the bed. "Let's get crackin'!"

"I have a question..."

"Shoot."

"You asked me if I ever killed anyone, remember?"

"S'right, I did."

"How 'bout you?"

"...Only when the need be."

"How often did the need be?"

"Not often enough."

"What does that mean?"

"Means that there was two or three of'em that got away with more'n they should have."

Bob finished buttoning up the back of Boudine's dress, as she completed closing up the front. She then pulled on her boots that were hidden from view when she stood and the hem of the dress fell to the floor. Boudine put on the long bonnet and tied the bow under her chin. "What do you think?" she asked.

As Bob tucked his shirt into his pants and buckled his belt, he looked at Boudine for a moment then said to her, "It's a little crazy soundin', but it might just work."

"Damned right it might work! They'll all be lookin' for a bandit with a black mustache and his partner who'll be wearin' a black scarf mask, not a gambler and his little bride. Now, let's get somthin' to eat, I'm famished. I swear, I could eat a whole cow."

"Together?"

"What do you mean, together? Sure thing, together. We got to get folks around here used to seein' us *together*," she emphasized.

A low rumbling and commotion came from outside. Bob went to the window that overlooked the street below. "Well, I'll be..." he muttered.

"What?" Boudine asked.

"Lookit down there," Bob indicated. Boudine went over beside Bob at the window and looked down.

"That's the U. S. Army Calvary," she announced.

"Sure looks like it."

"Wonder what the hell they're doin' here."

"Ain't that Custer ridin' in the lead there? I've seen his likeness in the newspaper before." Bob said.

"Yeah, that's him in the flesh. He and a gang of'em came to one of our shows quite a while back. He talked a bunch to Bill Cody and Hickok."

"Did you meet'im?"

"Just a little. He said I was a good shot. That was about it. He seemed more interested in Calamity Jane, as I recall."

"This might not be the best place to conduct our new business after all," Bob pondered.

"Are you joshin' me? When d'you ever come up against a soldier who could draw a winnin' hand, huh?" she walked away from the window, then added, "Like shootin' fish in a barrel... Let's eat."

Bob, in his gambling duds, and Boudine dressed in her buttoned-up dress with the long bonnet hiding her face, emerged from the hotel onto the boardwalk in front. They watched, along with other curious folks, as the last of the long line of U.S. Army supply wagons, chuck wagons and field cannons rumbled by, followed by the full regiment of mounted infantry and Indian scouts, heading due north out of town. "Wonder where they're headed?" Bob uttered to Boudine.

A man standing just to the right of Bob answered his question, "It's Custer's Seventh Cavalry. They're headed for Montana, one of'em said when I asked. Some place called Little Bighorn. Must be fixin' to go after the Sioux, I suspect."

"Thank you, sir," Bob said with a smile and touched two fingers to his *Boss of the Plains* hat. He then politely offered his arm to Boudine who slipped her arm in his as they headed up the boardwalk away from the other spectators.

"There's two-three ways to go here," Boudine said to Bob in a hushed tone, leaning toward him over the small table for two by the window of a rather nice, clean restaurant where they waited for their meal to be served.

"They've got a big bank right in the center of town here which means there'll be gold shipments in and out. Probably in the Monitor."

"Monitor?" Bob asked.

"S'a stagecoach built out of ship timbers with little gun windows for the inside guards," she told Bob.

"I'll be. Never saw one of'em before."

"Only a few around. Built to carry hundreds of pounds of gold. Wild Bill rode shotgun on'em for a bit between shows. Paid pretty good, he told me."

"How do we go about this if they have guards on the outside and the inside?"

"Shoot the horses first, then pick off the outside guards from a hideaway and wait all quiet for the ones inside to get all upset and want to get out."

Bob just stared into the darkness of Boudine's long bonnet... *Who the hell was this woman?...*

After a moment, Bob leaned in closer, "I told you I've never killed anyone before..."

The slatted long bonnet shook its head from side to side, then, "Look, Slye..."

"Duncan! Dammit," Bob scolded in a hushed harsh voice.

"Okay, Duncan-Dammit, I'll do the shootin' an' I won't kill'em. Just wing'em if they get brave an' then run the horses off. That suit'cha? Anyway, murderin' ain't somethin' I have a shine for, if that makes you feel better."

A young serving girl, with a crisp white apron over a light blue cotton ankle-length dress, brought over a tray of food and set the plates in front of each of them.

Boudine kept her long bonnet looking down and her hands folded in front of her, as if getting ready to say a prayer of Grace.

When the serving girl left, Bob uttered, "You said two or three ways..."

The long bonnet looked up slowly. From within came, "The bank or... the train."

After a moment, Bob took up his fork and knife and started to eat. Boudine did the same. Only the murmur of the other diners and the tinkle of glasses and dishes could be heard...

"See that man straddled on the rails up over the chute? The one with the spear?" Bob asked Boudine. "That was me." They were standing at the corral nearest to the slaughterhouse, as several cowboys who whistled, shouted and slapped their chaps at the petrified steers drove a small herd that had been cut from the larger cattle pens, toward the narrow killing chute.

Boudine watched through her slatted long bonnet as the man above the chute drove the killing spear down into the neck of a thrashing trapped steer, severing its spinal cord. The mortally wounded animal let out a loud gut-wrenching bawl and crashed to the ground with its legs rigid and twitching straight out from its body. Two men quickly opened the chute gate and hitched a block and tackle around the dead animal's horns, then reined the workhorse forward to pull the animal out of the chute and over to the slaughterhouse and into the skinning area inside, where men with sharp knives were feverishly beheading and skinning the fresh bodies. Just as quickly, another block and tackle team replaced it for the next kill.

Piles of hides were everywhere ready for the leather workers to continue the process.

"It stinks here," Boudine muttered from inside her bonnet and waved away the swarms of black flies.

"Yes it does." Bob answered flatly.

They turned and walked away.

"Was that answer enough for you?"

"I suspect it was."

"I had two choices. Stay on the homestead with no money and no future or head to somewhere else and try my luck."

"How long were you in Wichita?"

"Long enough to know killin' cattle wasn't what I wanted to do."

"Why didn't you go into the Army? You was right there at Fort Randall."

"I saw too much goin' on there. I saw soldiers brought in with their arms and legs all shot up with arrows and gunshot. I saw'em with their eyes hangin' out. I saw the doctors cuttin' off their limbs with a saw and them screamin' all bloody hell."

"How old were you?"

"Not old enough."

"But, there's other ways of workin' and makin' money."

"Not as fast and not enough for what I need."

"Why do you need it so fast?"

"Because, my aim is to get my mother into a proper house before she dies out there on that godforsaken homestead."

"But, from the sound of things, she seems pretty strong-willed.

"Stubborn as her mule's more like it. No, more so. If'n she don't die from the winter or roast in the summer heat, there's a good chance some renegades will end up burnin' her out. She's pretty handy with a rifle, but no match for an attack."

"Thought you said she has an Army friend."

"She does. But, he only comes around when he's not out on an expedition. No tellin' when his time'll be up or he's felled by an arrow or a musket."

"Does she know what you do for your keep?"

"I think she might suspect somthin', but she's never said nothin'."

"You really care for her, don't you, Slye?"

"She's the only thing between me and hell."

The saloon and gambling hall was a much more respectable situation than Deadwood or pretty much anywhere else where Bob had applied his card playing skills. The bar had the golden sheen of being carved and built by an artisan. The bartender had on a crisp white shirt and fancy black vest with gold stripes woven into it. The glasses of whiskey were the best money could buy and by no means watered down. The piano player played softly in the background and, the ladies who waited for a customer were certainly a cut above anything that was being offered in the Wild West gold mining towns.

Bob sipped a drink alone at the long bar and watched as Boudine, dressed in her men's working attire, studied the hand she'd just been dealt at the poker table nearest to him. Her hat was pulled down so's not to give the other players much to look at. Also, she had buttoned her shirt sleeves tightly around her wrists. Boudine was playing a smart game. Letting just enough hands go by so's not to bring any suspicion upon her.

The predetermined signals between Bob and Boudine had been rehearsed and were working. Bob's keen eye at counting cards was paying off, as he sent a subtle signal – hand on his whiskey glass – to Boudine to let the hand go and toss in her cards. The next hand she held onto, as Bob rested his arm on the bar, not touching the glass, and Boudine upped the ante and eventually gathered in a healthy pot.

This went on until a player gave up his spot at the table and walked away in disgust. Bob walked over, took the empty chair, and began to play. Boudine retreated to the bar with her winnings and watched as Bob went about letting the small bets go and hauling in the big pots.

For two consecutive nights they plied their trade, until one of the regular gamblers became suspicious and confronted Bob, who had accumulated another large pot in front of him. "You sure've been havin' a run of good luck there, mister. What'd you say your name is?"

Bob continued to look at the hand he held without looking up. "I didn't say."

"Well, I like to know who I'm playin' with. What's your name?"

"If it pleases you, sir, the name's Bob Duncan from over Fort Randall way."

"Well, you're a long ways off the beaten path. Ain't you, Bob Duncan."

Bob indicated the ante, "I believe the bet's to you, sir," Bob said without raising his voice or giving any indication that he was annoyed with the man's attitude.

"And I believe you're a fuckin' cheat!" the man shouted out.

Bob slowly looked up from his cards and gave the man a cold blue-eyed stare. He also let his left hand ease down to the Civil War derringer he kept in the rim of his boot whenever he gambled.

At the bar, Boudine sipped her drink and rested her hand on her holstered pistol. The other gamblers in the house all were silent and watching the altercation.

Bob stared at the gambler and smiled as he said, "It's your bet, sir."

"You're a cheatin' sumbitch! Show me your goddamned hand!"

"I believe it's your bet, sir," Bob repeated flatly.

Suddenly, the gambler reached for his sidearm and drew. In that instant, the discharge from Bob's derringer sent a lead slug right between the man's legs. The gambler froze for a moment, his eyes wide with the horror that had just happened. Then the shock hit him full-force and he fell over backwards in his chair, grasping his bleeding crotch and screaming in excruciating pain. Bob looked at the other astonished players at the table and turned over his cards. A royal flush. The others folded and Bob gathered up the pot, left the table and walked out of the saloon without another word. From the bar, Boudine quietly watched the commotion going on around the wounded gambler, then finished her drink and left.

"Jesus, even I didn't see that comin'! I didn't know you

carried a derringer!"

"You never accused me of cheatin' at cards."

"Guess I'd better be more careful around you there, Slye."

"Guess you'd better, Boudine."

"We have a fairly peaceful city here in Yankton, Mister Duncan, and we like to keep it that way."

"Yessir, I understand," Bob said to County Sheriff Zachary Conklyn, who was seated behind his orderly desk in his tidy office at the Yankton County Sheriff's Headquarters. There was not a gun case or even a gun in sight. He leaned forward and addressed Bob, who sat with his *Boss of the Plains* hat in his lap, in a straight-back chair opposite the sheriff's desk.

"That fella you shot last evening, and rightfully so from what all the others have told me who witnessed the ruckus. Well, he's a rather troublesome sort and probably had it coming to him. Doctor says he'll live if'n he doesn't get the infection. Probably won't be pleasing the ladies for quite some time though I suspect. But, as I said, we're proud of keeping the peace around here in Yankton. The President of the United States chose our city as the Capital of the Dakotas for that reason, among others. So, a word to the wise should be sufficient there, Mister Duncan."

"I appreciate your words, Sheriff, thank you."

"How long are you in town for?"

"Another day or two. We're... I'm just passing through these parts on my way north to set up a homestead."

The sheriff, a rather slim chap, clean-shaven with

a neatly trimmed mustache, but with the eyes and manner of a professional lawman, said to Bob, "You said 'we', sir."

Bob didn't hesitate. "My wife is with me, sir. We just said our vows only two weeks ago. I guess I'm not used to it yet."

The sheriff nodded with a slight laugh, "Well, you better get used to it, Mister Duncan, or you might catch what-for."

"I'll take your advice, Sheriff."

"Is gamblin' your occupation, Mister Duncan?"

"Not really, sir, but it does fill in the cracks from time to time."

The sheriff's eyes narrowed a bit. "What is it you do mainly, if I might ask?"

"I'm a writer of stories about the Western Frontier, sir."

The sheriff raised his eyebrows and studied Bob. "Is that right? My goodness. I never would've thought that. I read some of those dime novels, when I have some time to myself. Maybe, I've read some of yours, Mister Duncan."

Without a blink, Bob said, "That's quite possible, sir."

"My favorite is the Beadle's *Malaeska, the Indian Wife of the White Hunter*. You read that one?"

"Yessir, I have read that one. Many times."

"*Seth Jones* is a good one, too. *The Captives of the Frontier...*"

"Yessir, that is a good one, as well."

"Well, now, Mister Duncan, maybe you'll make me famous," the sheriff said with a grin.

Bob said, "It is a possibility, sir."

The sheriff paused, then said to Bob, "Duncan... Duncan..." he pondered, "Don't recall seein' your name on any of the books I've read."

Bob had an easy answer ready. "That's because most of the publishers back East don't use the real names of the writers."

With that, Sheriff Conklyn stood up from his chair and offered his hand over his desk. Bob rose and shook the sheriff's hand. "One bit of advice, Mister Duncan..."

"Yessir?"

"The man you shot has a brother and some friends who are a rather nasty lot. You should be careful and be on the lookout, just in case they come callin'."

Bob hesitated at the office door, then said, "I will do that, Sheriff. Thank you."

Bob turned to leave. The sheriff continued with, "Shame about Wild Bill Hickok. Did you hear?"

Bob turned back in the doorway, rather puzzled by the sheriff's remark. "Yessir, it is."

The sheriff mused, "Damned fine shooter he was…"

"So I've heard."

"He's been the subject of some of those dime novels I've read... You ever run into him in your writin' travels there, Mister Duncan?"

Bob paused for a second, then answered. "Only so much as a card game one night over in Deadwood, and a short conversation on the day he was shot."

Surprised, the sheriff said, "Really? You were there when it happened?"

"Nossir. I had left Deadwood just prior to the shootin'."

"You mean 'we' don't you, Mister Duncan?"

"Sir?" Bob answered quizzically.

"You mean 'we' meaning you and your new bride there, Mister Duncan."

"Oh, yessir, I mean 'we'. I'm going to have to do better on that one."

"You sure as hell are, Mister Duncan. If'n you want to keep your head intact," the sheriff said with a chuckle. "By the way, it looks like we'll be seein' to it that Wild Bill's killer will be gettin' his comeuppance right here in Yankton."

"Sir?"

"We just got notice that they've arrested the killer..." The sheriff looked at a note on his desk... "A Jack McCall. You ever run into'im over there in Deadwood, Mister Duncan?"

Bob did his best to hide his growing uneasiness with Sheriff Conklyn's continued questions. "Matter of fact, I was in a card game with both of'em the night before over at the Nuttal & Mann's Saloon."

"Really? Well, if that don't beat all. What was this Jack McCall like, Mister Duncan? I wouldn't mind knowing somethin' about'im, a'fore he arrives here, if you don't mind, sir."

Bob hesitated, then, "Far as I could tell, he was a terrible card player and drank more than his share of whiskey. Hickok had nearly cleaned him out before I entered the game. He left in a bad way."

The sheriff paused and then said, "Well, sir, he'll be escorted here to the capital for a trial and, I assume, a hangin' will follow."

That's good news, sir. Glad to hear it."

"I heard that ol' Hickok was done-up and down to his last blanket."

"I wouldn't know about that, sir. He seemed in pretty good spirits when I left him."

"Ya-know, it's always interested me how folks like this Jack McCall feel it's fine to carry out somethin' like that and think they'll get away with it, when the odds are stacked against'em that they won't."

Bob nodded, still standing at the half-open office door. The sheriff continued, "Problem with that is, there's usually someone like me around to step in and equalize the situation, Mister Duncan." The sheriff paused and kept his eyes on Bob, then broke into a grin. "Well, listen to me just runnin' off at the mouth. I'm sure you have plenty to do to get ready for your trip north. Good day to you, sir, and give my best to your bride."

"Thank you, sir, I will surely do that."

Just then, a deputy came hustling in past Bob and whispered something to the sheriff who quickly took out a holstered revolver from a desk drawer and strapped it on, then hurried after the deputy who brushed by Bob in the doorway. As the sheriff retreated, he said to Bob, "One thing about the law business, there's always a wrong doer just around the next corner. Good luck to you, Mister Duncan. With that, Sheriff Conklyn was gone...

Bob walked down the hallway toward his hotel room. He stopped in front of the closed door to

Boudine's room and looked up and down the corridor, saw that he was alone and tapped lightly on the door. He listened for movement inside. There was none to be heard. He tapped again. Still no answer. Bob turned away and continued down the hallway.

The first thing Bob noticed when he entered his hotel room was a copy of the *Press & Dakotan* newspaper on the bed. Obviously, Boudine had been in the room and left it there. Bob picked up the paper and read the headline on the front page that included a likeness of the outlaw Jesse James along with the story...

"Jesse James and his band of outlaws held up the Northfield Minnesota Bank and may be headed toward Yankton. Two members of the outlaw band were killed. A Charlie Pitts and a Bill Chadwell. Also, another bandit was wounded and has been identified as Frank James, the brother of Jesse James. Also, there may be members of the Younger Band among them. A posse, headed by American Express Company Detective Larry Hazen has been dispatched to apprehend the outlaws. The citizenry of Yankton are being asked to be on the lookout for any suspicious characters and to report such actions to the law immediately. Wanted posters have been distributed offering a $5000 reward for the capture or killing of Jesse James and his gang. A shoot to kill order has been issued."

Bob stopped reading and set the paper down. He pulled the gold pocket watch from his pocket and read the time. It was well after noon. *Where the hell was*

Boudine?...

The hardware supply company, set out amongst the other Yankton businesses on the main street, advertised on a sign hung on the front of the building that windows and doors were made-to-order. Bob had entered the store and was going about ordering a window and frame from the proprietor. "How long will it take to deliver the window to Fort Randall?"

The proprietor looked down a printed schedule of stage runs to the area and replied, "All else being equal, be about two to three weeks, since you're not ordering any special dimensions and just need a standard frame and window. Will there be someone there at the fort who will be expecting the delivery, sir?"

"Yessir, that would be a Master Sergeant William H. Bartholomew." Bob handed the proprietor a sealed letter envelope with the sergeant's name written on it. "If you would be so kind as to include this with the delivery, I'd be most appreciative."

"Of course, I'll see that it's put into the shipping box myself." The proprietor then filled out the rest of the billing receipt and handed it to Bob. "This includes the shipping costs."

Bob looked it over, then took the leather pouch out of his pocket and retrieved one of the gold coins he had relieved the highwayman of back outside of Scooptown. "This should cover it."

"Well, sir, that's more than enough. I'll get you your..."

Bob interrupted him with, "That won't be necessary, sir. If'n it's over the amount, then keep the rest for yourself for all the effort you're goin' to."

"Thank you, sir, that's most generous. I'll see to all the business myself and make sure everything's taken care of.

"I should probably include some extra panes of glass," Bob mused aloud.

"Three are included, sir. It's a long trek over there to Fort Randall."

"Well, thank you, sir. That should do it then."

"Is there a place in town where I can contact you and let you know when we get it over to the stage depot for delivery?"

"Nossir, I'm only in town for a day or two. Thank you again."

"Much obliged. Safe travels."

Bob touched the brim of his *Boss of the Plains* hat and left.

Out on the boardwalk, Bob looked up and down the street, but didn't see any sign of Boudine, either in her long bonnet and dress or her business clothes. He looked at his gold pocket watch and headed back to his hotel.

"Where the hell've you been, Boudine?" Bob demanded as he closed his hotel room door behind him.

Boudine was stretched out on the bed fully clothed in her men's work clothes, boots and all. She held in her hands a crumpled sheet of paper, which she offered to Bob without a word, as she swung her legs over the side with more than a little contempt. Bob took the paper, straightened it out and looked at it. It was a wanted poster that read:

REWARD – DEAD OR ALIVE!
$5000
for Robbing the Northfield Minnesota Bank.
They are believed to be Jesse James and his Gang.
Also, possibly members of the Younger Band.
SHOOT TO KILL!

Bob looked up from reading the poster and asked, "Where'd you get this?"

Boudine's jaw was really working and she was sniffing more than usual. "I was over t'the train depot sizin' things up for us, when the train comes in all the way from Minnesota, and a bunch of American Express agents come leapin' outta two boxcars with their horses and started handin'em out and nailin'em up around."

"What does that have to do with us?"

Boudine looked straight at Bob. "It don't. It has to do with *me*." She then put her hand on the *Press & Dakotan* newspaper on the bed where Bob had left it. "J'you read this?"

"Yes..."

"I was supposed to be on that raid."

Bob just stared at her with a bewildered look on his face, without saying anything. Boudine got up off the bed and went to the window, wiping her nose on her shirtsleeve.

"Are you going to tell me what this is all about?"

Boudine stared out the window. "A while back, I met up with Jesse and some of his band. It was shortly after I left the Wild West Show. Sumbitch, Charlie Pitts, had takin' a likin' to me after comin' to one of my last shows and was followin' me around for a bit. All the time, tryin' to get into my knickers. But, I held'im off. He kept tellin' me that he was a member of the James Gang, which I did not believe one scrap until he took me to meet Jesse and Frank James at a secret hideout..."

She hesitated for a moment. "Well?" Bob said.

"Well, we all were drinkin' pretty much and Charlie Pitts puts up a bet that I could out-shoot anyone in the gang and one thing led to another."

"Go on..."

She turned from the window and folded her arms across her chest and challenged, "You seen me shoot. What do you think?"

"Charlie Pitts won the bet?"

"You bet your jolly-stick he did!"

"I still don't see how this has anything to do with us," Bob said as he went to the bed and picked up the newspaper to have another look at the report.

"Well, they all thought it was a hoot, 'cept for Jesse who got all dark and broody. Then, Charlie Pitts starts comin' after me real hard, so's I offered him a proposition. If'n he gets Jesse to let me be part of their next big plan, then I'd let'im lay me all he wanted."

Bob looked up from the newspaper and indicated the story, "This Charlie Pitts?"

"Yeah, that Charlie Pitts."

"He's dead."

"Yup, deader than the skunk that he was. I was supposed to be on that raid in Northfield. It was all agreed upon, but then, Frank and Jesse and Cole Younger got into a big argument and I was told to skedaddle. Seems Jesse was the boss of it all and what he said was what was done."

Bob indicated the paper again, "Your name could've been in here, too."

"Maybe, maybe not," she pondered.

Bob put the paper down and sat on the bed. "Where've you been? We were supposed to meet up at the restaurant after I was done meeting at the sheriff's office."

"I went lookin' for that rat Jesse James?"

"You what?" Bob remarked incredulously.

"The American Express agents that was puttin' up them wanted posters got word that Jesse was about and gave chase. I saddled up and rode out after'em."

Bob could not believe what he was hearing. His mouth literally hung open. He began to stutter, "You... you did... did what?"

"I chased after the posse because they were askin' for volunteers to help corral Jesse."

"Are you full-up crazy? They could just as well be chasin' after us!"

"I wanted to see for myself that they got Jesse James. That's what it was."

"Just because he didn't want you along for that bank raid?"

"That and the fact that he didn't want me along because I was a woman and because I was a better shot than any of'em. Also, that he couldn't care less about that son-of-a-dog Charlie Pitts gettin' after me. The sumbitch thought it was funny and kept tellin' Pitts to hog-tie me and throw me down like a calf!" She sniffed and wiped her nose on her sleeve.

Bob waited a moment, then asked, "Did they

catch'im?"

"Jesse?"

"Yeah."

"Nope. The posse chased after'im all the way to what's called Devil's Gulch above Split Rock Creek and, just as they were bearin' down on'im, he ran his horse full-on and jumped the gorge. I saw it with my own eyes and couldn't believe he made it over. Looked like it must've been close to twenty foot across."

Bob sighed. Silence filled the small hotel room. "You hungry?" Bob finally asked.

"Yes. I'll go change into my woman tent."

"...There's 'nother reason for me wantin' to see Jesse James get his..."

"What's that?"

"...After I left the hideout, Jesse done followed after me on the trail and threw me down and had his way with me. When he was done, he laughed and spit on me and left me there on the ground... I hope when they hang'im, his head is pulled clean off!"

"I figure the train might be a good plan for us," Boudine said in a hushed voice, as she leaned over her dinner plate at the same restaurant they had eaten at previously.

Bob leaned closer to her slatted long bonnet and said, "That's not somethin' I'm familiar with. I'm just not sure..."

"Look, all you have to do is go on up the tracks about ten miles or so and lay down a tree across'em. I'll be on the train. You be there with the horses. When it stops, you jump on board with your Winchester and fire a warning shot to scare the passengers. I'll do the same and we start unloadin'em of their cash and valuables real quick. I already bought us some carpetbags."

"What about any guards?

"They usually only have guards on the boxcar carryin' the gold and money shipments. At least, that's what Wild Bill once told me. Seems he rode guard on some big shipments between times."

A serving girl brought over a water pitcher, filled their glasses and walked away.

"I still don't know about this. Seems stoppin' a stage'd be much easier and safer."

"Tell me something', Slye..."

"Duncan," Bob reminded.

Yeah-yeah. Tell me somethin'. You ever been on a train a'fore?" She asked so no one around could hear.

Bob hesitated, then, "...Once... Not in the train. I jumped on one headin' up to Wichita from down Texas way. Rode in an open cattle car 'til they found us and gave us the boot."

"Us?"

"Yeah, there were others ridin' the same way as me. Had to fight some of'em off tryin' to rob me."

"So, you ain't never rode inside a train a'fore."

"That's right."

"Well, the folks who ride trains got the money because it costs to ride'em. More'an the Wells Fargo Stage. They also tend to carry more valuables with'em such as jewelry and gold coins," she instructed. "It's just there for the takin'," she urged.

The serving girl arrived and set down their meals.

"You that bastard who shot my brother?" someone groused, standing right next to Bob and Boudine's table.

They both looked up. Boudine, not letting her slatted long bonnet open. Bob looked right into the glaring eyes of a burly, unshaven man with a large black mustache.

"Sir?" he questioned.

"I says, are you the one what shot up my brother over'ta the saloon last night?" he repeated in a threatening tone. There were two other no less ominous men standing behind him. All wore six-shooters strapped to their waists.

Bob answered easily in a nonthreatening manner, "If you mean the one who was drunk and losin' at poker and drew down on me, then you are correct, sir."

The man rested his hand on his holstered pistol. "Step outside!"

Bob took his napkin and wiped his mouth. "My wife and I haven't finished our meal here, sir. Once we do, I'll be happy to accommodate you."

The man leaned over Bob with a mean scowl and said, "I said right now, you stinkin' piece of goat shit an' leave your whore where she is!"

Bob set the napkin down on the table without taking his hand off of it. He gave bonnet-hooded Boudine a hidden wink and said easily, "You should never have said that about my wife, sir. Now, we'll just have to make amends." With that, Bob flipped the white napkin up into the man's face and instantly drew his Peacemaker up and onto the man's forehead as he stood up and cocked the hammer back. The man behind him started for his six-shooter. Boudine was already in motion with her fork, which she expertly swung up under the man's chin, stabbing him through his flesh and tongue and planting the tines right into the roof of his mouth. She continued the motion by bending the fork handle up over his chin and mouth with the heel of her hand. She then shoved him hard into the second man, who was fumbling for his gun, knocking him to the ground. With the wounded man gurgling blood and in extreme pain, Boudine reached up under the skirt of her dress and drew a derringer from her boot, aiming it at both the men. Bob eased back his Peacemaker and told the mustached brother, "We're leavin' here now. I suggest that you take your friend there over to a doctor before he bleeds to death. And, if you're thinkin' of followin' us, I suggest you think better of it. All the folks here are witness to your actions and the good sheriff already warned me to look out for you gentlemen and is aware that you might be up to doin' this. So, goin' to him might not get you what you want."

Only the low golden glow of the oil lamps from the street below illuminated the two glistening bodies entwined on the bed in Bob's hotel room. Both Bob and Boudine reached the height of their enjoyment at the same time and let go with the sounds of complete fulfillment. Bob rolled onto his back and caught his breath, then said to Boudine, "You never told me you had a derringer."

"You never called me a whore." After a moment, Boudine uttered, "How'd'ya'like bein' married there, Slye?"

Bob answered, a bit breathless, "What?"

"Hell, you say it enough; people are goin' to believe it."

"I think that be the idea, Boudine."

"Just as long as it's just that and nothin' more."

"Right."

"Nothin' about bein' married to a man has ever interested me."

"Okay."

"Bein' tied up with kids and cookin' and washin' clothes ain't somethin' I see in my future. So don't go gettin' no ideas just because we been layin' together from time to time."

Bob sighed, "I won't."

"Good."

The dawn broke over the frontier town of Yankton. The hustle and bustle of the day's business had already begun. Both the Bandit Bob Slye and the Bandit Sally Mae Boudine had paid up their stay at the hotel and left – separately.

Bob had departed before sunrise, taken both his horse and Boudine's from the livery, and headed out to follow the train tracks north, with a planned stop about ten miles out. Boudine had headed to the depot and purchased a ticket for the train. Their plan was in motion.

Hidden from view in a clump of trees and shrubs near the railroad tracks, Bob finished changing into his working clothes and affixed the black mustache to his upper lip. Then, after applying the white stage makeup to the roan's forehead, he made sure the two horse's reins were secured to a tree branch and headed out of the brush to where he had already placed a felled cottonwood across the railroad tracks. The train would give him plenty of warning because of the noise of the engine and the belching black smoke from its boiler.

Aboard the fully booked Central Pacific train heading to all points west, Boudine nonchalantly walked through the several passenger cars, sizing up the different types of travelers and noting what they might be carrying; and occasionally wiping her nose on her sleeve. With her hat pulled down, so's not to draw attention to herself, she also looked out for who might be carrying a weapon.

Back in her seat, where she had deposited several bundled up carpetbags, she slumped down and pretended to snooze...

"I'm not so all-fired sure about this, Boudine. It seems a might bigger situation than either of us has been up to as yet."

"Look, you ain't never going to get that big place for your ma if'in you don't take a big chance. We can go around pickin' off stagecoaches forever and never catch the big fish."

"Yes, but tryin' to catch a whale with a Peacemaker don't sound very smart."

"If you shoot the whale in the eye it is! Now, are you in or out? We can go 'round and 'round all day findin' ways not to do this. If you're not wantin' to do it, then tell me now, so's we don't waste any more time jabberin'. In or out?"

"In."

A turkey vulture circled high above in the near cloudless sky. *Not a good sign*, Bob thought to himself. But, then he thought of his mother out on that thankless homestead, especially with news of recent Sioux activity thereabouts. And, the fact that Bob had been considering that the business of robbing stagecoaches might not be something he wanted to pursue for a lifetime, made him think that this undertaking might just do the trick. *"Just once, he thought, just this one time..."*

The train wrenched hard and the iron wheels screeched on the rails, as the brakes ground the train toward a full stop. *"Bob had done his job,"* Boudine thought as she reached into one of the carpetbags and wrapped a gloved hand around the old LaMat Grape Shot revolver, she had lifted from the dead road agent on the trail out of Scooptown. Unbeknownst to the other passengers, she readied it on the seat. With everyone distracted and wondering what was going on, Boudine quickly pulled the black silk mask out of her pocket and pulled it over her head, then put her hat back on.

The screeching iron wheels sprayed a shower of hot sparks, as the belching black steam train slid along the tracks to a grinding stop, just before its giant cowcatcher rammed into the felled tree that Bob had thrown down. Bob quickly ran up to the side of the engine, grabbed onto a handle and leaped up into the open cab with his Winchester '73 leveled at the wide-eyed engineer, whose gloved hands were still straining on the brake handle. A young fireman, braced against the coal tender, immediately grabbed his coal shovel and threw it at Bob, just missing his head. It clanged off the boiler as Bob, wearing his black mustache and green glasses, whirled, aimed his rifle right between the eyes of the panicked young man, and motioned both to raise their hands. "Where's your weapon?" Bob gritted at the engineer in a hushed rasp of a voice that he thought might help further his disguise.

"There," the engineer pointed to a small storage shelf that held a six-shooter. Bob reached over, took the gun out, and shoved it into his gun belt. "Any guards travelin' on this train?"

"Don't know."

Bob drew back the hammer on his Winchester with a menacing click.

"Maybe...yes..." the engineer blurted out nervously.

"How many?" Bob demanded.

"Two." The engineer's face had gone ashen.

"Get off and run for your life!" Bob commanded. The two men froze. "Now!"

Both the engineer and the fireman leaped down out of the cab and scampered away as fast as they could. Then, Bob heard a gunshot from inside one of the train cars...

The bullet had just snapped right by Boudine's ear and exploded the oil lamp over the seat behind her. She ducked again, as an American Express agent aimed and fired a second shot, just missing her right shoulder. Most of the passengers were hunkered down in their seats. A woman screamed in panic. Boudine winged the agent in each shoulder with her King-Queen-Ace shots from her Colt. Only this time, she left off the *Ace*, which was a good thing for the agent. The two bullets each ripped out the seams of the agent's coat sleeves at the shoulder points and caused just enough pain to put him out of commission. Then, with the LaMat Grape Shot in her left hand, she aimed at the roof and pulled the trigger on the shotgun blast that blew a hole right on through the wood paneled ceiling. A woman screamed again. The agent slid down the closed passenger car door and slumped onto his rump on the floor. The woman continued to scream, until, "Stop your fuckin' screamin' a'fore I shut your mouth for'ya!" Boudine shouted in her best man's voice to the frenzied woman, as she pointed the LaMat right at her black-dressed-cinched-up waist. That did it. Boudine kept the LaMat leveled as she holstered her Colt. "Now, here's what's gonna happen. I'm gonna open this here carpetbag and y'all are gonna empty your valuables into it. And, if'in I see anyone holdin' back or if'in I see anyone try to get funny with a gun, the next hole I blow open with this will be in y'all."

The rifle blast from behind Boudine stunned everyone. Boudine whirled around to see a man's six-shooter catapult from his hand. The bullet had ricocheted off the pistol chamber, sending it crashing against a window, shattering it into a thousand pieces. Immediately, Boudine saw that it was Bob who had shot the pistol out of the second American Express agent's hand. The agent grabbed his injured hand in pain. Boudine leveled the LaMat Grape Shot at the agent's gut. "Get your sorry ass over there and sit down next to your friend," Boudine ordered the agent. With Bob prodding him with his Winchester '73 in his back, the man quickly obliged. Then, Boudine announced to the passengers, as she menaced them with the wicked looking LaMat in her left hand, "Now, that will be enough of that. The next one what tries to interfere with our business here gets a load right square in the middle. The quicker we get it done, the quicker y'all can be on your way. And another thing, there's four of us on this train, so don't go makin' fools of yourselves. You want to die, that's your choice to make."

Bob gave her a slightly puzzled look. She nodded her head toward the next coach. Bob picked up a carpetbag and headed through the door to the next car...

"Four of us?"
"You sayin' there weren't?"
"Yes, I'm sayin' there weren't."
"Did they know that?"
"...No..."
"Well, there'ya go then."
"That LaMat Grape Shot had only one load in it."
"Did they know that?"
"...No..."
"Well, there'ya go then."

With two full to overflowing carpetbags attached to the pommels of their saddles, the horses strained a bit under the weight of the loot Bob and Boudine had relieved from the train passengers. They had traveled an additional ten miles or so before coming upon the possible hiding place they had staked out on their earlier ride in from Scooptown.

MILLIE MAE DUNCAN

EIGHT

The snow that roared in with a vengeance overnight was blocking the thick pine board door to Millie Mae Duncan and her son Bob's sod house. Bob shoved hard against the stubborn hindrance until he was able to produce an opening just wide enough for him to squeeze through. Although the snowstorm had stopped for the time being, the morning sun's bright light, shining across the pure white landmass, nearly blinded him for a moment. Outside it was bone cold, as wind gusts swirled around the small sod home. Millie Mae handed Bob the shovel from within and he started clearing the head-high snowdrift away so the door could swing wide.

Even though the cold chilled him through, Bob was glad for the snow. He would have to stay at home to help his mother set about seeing to the animal's care and feeding to make sure they were able to survive the wretched freeze. More importantly, Bob would be forced not to have to attend Miss Lundergan's school for several days, which suited him just fine, being that he was still in a bit of a fit about what had happened the day before...

"Robert I will need you to stay behind this afternoon," Miss Lundergan had asked Bob, as the other students gathered their books and bundled up before filing outside for their trek along the wintery paths home.

"Yes, ma'am," Bob answered without hesitation. He was often asked to help because he had grown to be the tallest of the other boys and had paid enough attention to her lessons to have turned out to be the smartest of the homestead kids.

The door closed as the last pupil trooped out and disappeared. Marjorie Lundergan placed the wooden bar across the door and set it into its iron catches. No one could enter. She then turned to the two windows and drew the curtains, blocking out most of the late afternoon light.

"Robert, please put some wood on the fire," she said with assured ease.

Bob did as she asked. When he was finished stoking the fire in the small iron stove in the corner, he stood and faced his teacher ready for whatever help was needed.

She quietly set herself against the front edge of her desk table and placed her hands on either side of her. Her eyes softened as she spoke, "How old are you now, Robert?"

To Bob, she sounded much different now from when she was teaching the class. Bob cleared his throat, "Goin' on sixteen next, ma'am."

Marjorie looked at Bob for a moment. The flames from the new logs on the fire were heating up the room. "Are you familiar with girls yet, Robert?"

Bob hesitated for a moment. This was not what he had expected. "I guess so..."

"Have you been with a woman yet, Robert?"

Bob's mouth went dry, "I...I've..."

Marjorie smiled and tilted her head a bit. She reached up and removed the ornately carved tortoiseshell comb that held her upswept hair in place, letting her long brown locks drift down onto her shoulders. "Come closer, Robert," she uttered in almost a whisper.

Bob obeyed and stepped to within a yard of Miss Lundergan. She looked at him for a moment, then straightened up from the edge of the desk. "There comes a time for every young man when the act of being with a woman must first be taught." She said this as she stepped closer and reached for his hand, gently took it and brought it up to her; firmly pressing it over her heart... and did not let go...

"Wake up! Rise'n'shine!" came a loud voice ringing out of the void. "We gotta ways to go and it's your turn to drive the wagon."

Bob jerked his head up from a sound sleep on his bedroll. Boudine was already boiling up coffee and frying some quail eggs over their campfire. Bob looked around, gathering his thoughts...

"That must'a been some dream you was havin' there, Slye."

Bob sat up. "What?"

Boudine chuckled, "Hell, you was moanin' and groanin' like you was really pleasurin' someone."

Bob reached for his boots... "Damn," he muttered.

"I'd say you was dreamin' about me, but I ain't never heard you groan like that when we're..."

"Hey!" Bob snorted as he shoved his foot into a boot.

"Oh, I see. It really wasn't me you was dreamin' about. Must've been someone real special there, Slye."

Bob stood. "Will you stop that. I wasn't dreamin't'all."

"Could've fooled me there, Bob," Boudine baited. She then poured out two tin cups of coffee and handed one over to Bob. "Here, you'll be needin' this, Slye."

"Hey! I told'ja to stop callin' me that. I keep tellin'ya, it's Duncan. Dammit!"

"Okay, Duncan-Dammit. Hell, I know'd it'd just be a matter of time a'fore I caught you cheatin' on me," she teased with a snigger.

With Bob grumbling under his breath, they quickly finished eating and packed up the small covered wagon Boudine had dickered for on the outskirts of Scooptown upon their return. A down-and-out prospector, who didn't have a tail feather left, had even thrown in the two-mule team, based on some of the gold coins that Boudine had lifted from the train passengers and used to complete the transaction. Boudine's idea was to round up all of their hidden loot from the various places where they had each stashed it and consolidate their holdings into one central hideaway.

Bob had made meticulous notations in his leather-covered notebook that only made sense to him. That way, he would be the only one who could decipher the directions and whereabouts of his plunder, which he had hidden mainly under rocks and buried in scrub and log-covered holes. Boudine, on the other hand, had already secured most of her collections in a hidden cave at the edge of the Black Hills. They had come to an agreement that they would bring Bob's share to the cave for safekeeping and then divvy it up according to their understanding.

The caves were not an easy place to locate. They drove the small wagon across the open prairie expanse, at times cutting their own trail through the waves of grass. Herds of elk and buffalo grazed over the endless rolling hills by the hundreds. Mule deer ran off at the sight of the wagon lumbering along behind the two mules.

"How do you know we're headed in the right direction?"
"See them hills way off yonder?"
"Yes."
"That'd be where't'is."
"You're sure?"
"Listen for the sound of the wind. Then you'll know we're there."

Bob was on the driver's box. The two mules and their horses were the first to hear the distant rumble and started to buck and fidget about in their traces. Boudine reined up and listened for a moment. Bob pulled in the mules that were increasing their resistance against the harnesses. Boudine scanned the prairie. The rumbling was rapidly getting louder. The ground beneath them began to shake. Boudine shouted out to Bob, "Stampede!"

On the horizon from behind them, the ominous dark cloud of a thousand rampaging buffalo appeared. They were headed their way and would be on them in minutes. Boudine spotted an outcropping of a clump of trees and large boulders, two hundred yards off to their left. "BURN-THE-BREEZE!" She yelled over the approaching thunder and turned her horse in the direction of the boulders. Bob jerked the mule's reins and cracked the whip for them to follow. The sound of the approaching horde roared louder and louder. The earth beneath their thousands of pounding hooves throbbed out of control.

At the boulders, Boudine frantically tied off her horse and ran to help Bob pull the wagon and the panicked mules just inside the grove of trees. Bob then ran to the roan, hitched to the back of the wagon, and untied the reins. The horse tried to buck and pull away. Bob struggled mightily with the terrified animal and finally tied it to a tree. The deafening noise was almost upon them; Boudine drew her rifle out of its scabbard and ordered Bob to do the same. "Shoot the ones in front!" she shouted over the din. Bob immediately knelt, aimed his Winchester '73, and fired off shot after shot at the line of thundering buffalo. Boudine was right next to him and did the same. The animals they hit catapulted into the air and crashed to the ground. Instinctively, the stampeding herd parted around the dead and veered away. The more buffalo they felled, the wider the gap between them and the stampede. Choking dust enveloped the boulders and trees until neither Bob nor Boudine could see to shoot anymore. Then, as fast as the cloud of dust had appeared, it cleared. The entire mass had veered to the right and plowed over the prairie like a giant swirling tidal wave.

Bob stood and watched the receding storm. The threat had passed. He saw the pile of dead buffalo that had been sacrificed to divide the onslaught. The mules and horses began to calm down. As he started to brush the dust from his shirt and front of his pants, he heard Boudine... laughing... out loud. He looked over at her. She was seated on the ground, laughing louder and louder.

"What the hell're you laughing at? What's so damned funny, Boudine?"

As much as she tried, she couldn't stop. Just kept on laughing until she had to quit to even breathe. She staggered to her feet, a big grin still on her face, still sputtering with laughter. Tears streaked down her dust-caked cheeks.

"Whoa," she finally uttered, "I didn't think it would work..."

"Damn, girl, this ain't funny at all!" Bob said, annoyed as all hell.

"Shootin' them buffalo," she said between gasps for air, "never thought it'd work."

"What're you talkin' about?"

She held up her hand and took another breath, then said, "Buffalo Bill Cody tol' me that's what he done once to turn a stampede. Thought he was just givin' me a bunch'a cow flap. Never in a million did I think it'd work..."

Bob just stood there, not knowing if he should get mad or just smack her one. Boudine threw water on the fire by walking right up to Bob, wrapped her arms tight around his neck and kissed him long and deep, dust and all.

After a goodly amount of time, they brought the wagon up as close as possible to the rocky hill and woods-bound location. From there, they hauled several loads of their plunder in by horseback and then by foot. It had been a full two-day affair.

Amongst a rocky outcropping of boulders, low cliffs and compressed glacier rock, they came to a small rock-lined ravine. "This be it," Boudine announced and dumped her tied up cloth sacks onto the ground in front of an undersized natural opening in the rocks.

Bob set down his load and stared at the opening. "Hell, you say! That be no wider than the brim of my hat."

"Maybe a little bit more, but don't think any folks would want to venture into it."

"How'd you come upon this place, Boudine?" Bob asked.

"Lakota Injun who was with the Wild West Show tol' me about it. It's a sacred place they call *The Wind Cave*. Don't think any other white folk know about it."

"How'd he come to tell you?"

"He trusted me... let's leave it at that."

"What if he comes back upon it?"

"Can't see that happenin'."

"Why?"

"Broke his neck durin' the stampede act of the show."

Just then, a strong gust of wind seemed to whistle right out of the small mouth of the cave and snatch Bob's *Boss of the Plains* hat right off of his head and suck it back into the opening before he could grab it.

"Dammit!"

Boudine guffawed, "See I told'ja!" She then stepped to the opening in the rock. "Here, Slye, give me a hand," she asked as she began to descend down into the dark hole. "There's about a three foot drop, and then you scramble into the bigger part. That's where we'll stash the loot. Okay, let go." Bob let go of her hands and Boudine dropped down through the opening and disappeared for a moment. Then, she reappeared with Bob's hat and tossed it up to him. "Okay, I'm goin' down in. You drop the bags to me when I say so."

Boudine disappeared, then shouted, "Start droppin'."

Bob hefted one bag after another into the cave opening until they were all in, then peered into the hole. "Looks pretty dark in there," Bob said.

"Sun don't reach down here much."

After a few minutes, Boudine appeared and held up her hands. Bob grabbed hold and pulled her up and out. They went about this until all of their tied up sacks of loot were hidden.

"What if I have to go down in there?" Bob asked, as he pulled Boudine out for the last time.

"Don't get fat."

Toward evening, they drove the wagon back down the hills and across the plains to a spring surrounded by shrub and a cluster of cottonwoods that they had passed by on the way to the cave. There, they made camp, washed up, fed and watered the horses and the two mules, ate roasted fresh-killed rabbit and then, after a time, had their way with each other under a bright full moon...

"When's your birthday there, Slye?" Boudine asked, stretched out next to him on his bedroll.

"Why're you askin' "

"Curious, that's all. When is it?"

"Curiousity killed the cat."

"So I hear, but I ain't dead yet. So, when's your damned birthday?"

After a moment, Bob answered with, "Sometime in October. Why?"

"Sometime in October? Ain't there a particular day then?"

"I was born in a wagon on the way West. Sometime in October."

"So, when do you celebrate your birthday then? Any day in October you want?"

"Nearest my mother can remember 't'was around six of October. Least that's what she wrote down when I came on."

"Six of October then."

"Might be fifth or seventh..."

"Sixth! What t'was the year?"

"'Round eighteen-fif... Why're you so all fired up about when I was born?"

"Because, everyone needs to know the day they're born. It's the law."

Bob laughed out loud, "That's crazy, it ain't the law! You're just plain loony."

"I know... So, why don't'cha ask me when I was born then?"

"I don't really care..."

"Go ahead, ask me."

Bob sighed, "When were you born, Boudine?"

Very rapidly, she spit out, "August-eight-eighteen-fifty-five-at-eight-o'clock-sharp-on-a-stormy-night-with-big-bolts-of-lightning-strikin'-and-rollin'-thunderheads-clappin'-all-around."

"You don't say..."

"Yup, they sure as hell knew I had arrived."

They let the prairie breeze waft over their spent

bodies and lull them to sleep...

"I got me some business to do in Scooptown."

"What business?" Bob inquired, as he finished hitching the mules to the covered wagon.

"My business," Boudine said in a clipped way.

"Suit yourself," Bob said and went over to retrieve his horse from where he had laid the reins over a tree branch. "Your turn to drive," he added.

Bob mounted up. Boudine tied her horse to the back of the wagon, stepped up onto the driver's box, and slapped the reins onto the rumps of the mules.

As they started off in the direction of Scooptown, Bob noticed a flock of circling vultures overhead and was glad he wasn't a rotting carcass out on the South Dakota grassland.

"When we get to Scooptown, we should try and sell this rig. Too much for us to be haulin' around..."

"But, what about comin' back to the cave?" Bob asked.

"We'll just get ourselves 'nother one... One way or 't'other..."

Bob made a deal at the livery in Scooptown to have them sell the mules and the covered wagon for a fee that was agreeable. They also left their horses to be brushed down, fed and cared for.

"Why'n't you get us a room at the hotel, while I get done what I need to get done," Boudine suggested, as they left the livery and headed along the boardwalk of Scooptown, carrying their saddlebags and rifles with them.

Clouds began to roll in overhead and there was a chill in the air. "Comin' on winter, I suspect," Bob mentioned. "How long're you going to be?"

"'Bout an hour. Maybe less."

Bob crossed the muddy main street toward the same hotel and saloon he had stayed in before. But, he stopped at the front door and watched after Boudine, as she headed toward the end of town and turned the corner toward where Bob knew there were several Chinese business establishments. Mainly, laundries and a few shops, but also, a number of brothels and opium dens that were frequented by those in need of relief.

Bob thought about following Boudine, but pocketed the notion; knowing that if she spied him, it'd cause a row that he could do without. "*You never try and pet a cornered feral cat. It'll scratch your eyes out, sure as the Devil's in Hell,*" his mother used to tell him.

Bob bypassed the saloon and gambling tables and went straight to the hotel registry. The fresh wanted poster tacked on the wall beside the hotel reception desk startled Bob.

WANTED DEAD OR ALIVE!
$5000 REWARD – 2 TRAIN ROBBERS!
Wanted for robbing passengers on the northbound train out of
Yankton, South Dakota.
They are considered armed and dangerous!
SHOOT TO KILL!

"Nice to see you again, sir," the proprietor said with a smile from behind the reception desk.

Again, Bob was startled. "What?"

"Good to have you back, Mister Duncan. Will you be staying long?"

"Not long, but I'll need a room with two beds. I'm travelin' with a friend this time."

"Sure thing, Mister... it is Duncan, isn't it?"

"Yessir."

"We have a double room overlookin' the street. Will that do?"

"Fine..." He looked at the poster once again. There was a sketch of the two train robbers. One with a black mustache and dark glasses and the other with a black scarf wrapped around *his* face with eyeholes cut into it. Both were unrecognizable to anyone but Bob... Boudine was not going to like this.

Bob hastily stashed his saddlebags and Winchester '73 in the hotel room, locked the door and hustled back down the stairs and onto the street, taking the side door exit so's not to attract any attention in the lobby. He wanted to find Boudine before she saw the poster in the hotel. They needed a new plan...

Bob looked up and down the busy muddy street, with its constant passage of horses, oxen-drawn wagons and mules carrying prospector's supplies and tools of the trade. "Damn!" he said to himself and headed toward where he had seen Boudine turn off the main street.

The headline on a newspaper, left on a wooden bench outside a small eating establishment, caught his eye. Bob stopped and picked up the paper. "DARING

TRAIN ROBBERY NEAR YANKTON!" The words blared inside his head. The same sketches of the train robbers were printed over the report. It was then Bob realized this was not the first time he had seen a sketch of himself wearing the disguise of black mustache and military sunglasses. He was now wanted in several South Dakota territories. As his mouth went dry, Bob folded the newspaper and took it with him. *"Where the hell are you, Boudine?"*

The side street led to where most of the Chinese immigrant workers had been relegated, as their own segregated part of Scooptown. It was a gloomy, depressed place that featured two rows of shoddy buildings and tent fronts on either side of the garbage strewn dirt street. The shops, rooming houses and, what everyone knew were small brothels, gambling and opium dens, featured painted signs in Chinese characters. Very little English appeared anywhere, except for the word *"Laundry"* here and there. The local law did not reach this street. The immigrants had their own system of dealing with their own state of affairs. Something that the local sheriff and town bosses felt obliged to adhere to, given a regular participation in the fruits of their labors.

Bob looked into several of the shadowy and ominous establishments, averting the glazed, dead eyes of the wanton, overly white powdered-up women looking for a customer. His stomach recoiled from the squalor and putrid overhanging stench of the desperate and hopeless. No sign of Boudine anywhere. Exasperated, he turned back toward the main street.

Then, just before he reached the corner, a voice from behind him made him stop and turn around.

"Hey, Bob! Wait up." Boudine came hurrying diagonally across the rutted dirt street. A scrawny mongrel dog, trying to feed off a meatless bone scavenged from a heap of refuse, skittered out of her way. "What the hell're you doin' down here?" Her tone was quite harsh.

"I would ask you the same thing there, Boudine."

"I told'ja I had some business to take care of."

"What kind of business?"

"None of yours, that's for damned sure," she gritted.

Bob noticed something. "You got some white stuff on your nose there," he indicated. Boudine quickly wiped her nose on her sleeve and sniffed. Her eyes had gone black and glistened as she spoke.

"I asked you what you was doin' here, Slye!" she hissed.

"We got us a problem..."

They entered the hotel through the side entrance and hurried up the stairs to the room. Boudine dropped her saddlebags and rifle next to Bob's. He started to speak, "We'd better get the hell outta..."

"Shut the fuck up, Slye, an' let me think," Boudine shot back. Her eyes danced with anger. She paced the room like a caged panther. "We can handle this. We can handle this," she sputtered. "No one knows us here."

"They know me, Boudine. The manager remembered me from before and I'm sure they'd remember you if'n you set down at a card game."

"They don't remember me in a dress and bonnet, now would they, Slye?" she answered firmly.

"No..." Bob answered apprehensively.

"No is right. I'm the new wife, remember? Or have you forgotten that you're a married man?"

Bob stepped over to the bed nearest to him and sat down. He unfolded the newspaper that he still had tightly squeezed in his hand and stared at the drawings of the two train robbers.

Boudine stepped up in front of Bob and pulled the newspaper away from him, letting it flutter to the floor.

"What..."

She then sniffed, wiped her nose on her sleeve and started deliberately unbuttoning her shirt.

"What're you doin there, Boudine?"

"What a new wife should be doin', Slye," she answered with a grin. Her pupils were now fully black and sparkled in the late afternoon light that filtered through the white cotton curtains that covered the window. "And, I'm feelin' good, Slye. I'm feelin' real good."

The hotel manager nodded and smiled as Bob and Boudine, dressed in her dark brown floor-length dress and long bonnet, walked arm in arm toward the front door. Bob touched two fingers to his *Boss of the Plains* hat and nodded back.

As they passed by the hotel saloon and gambling hall, a young painted lady standing on the board walkway finished smoking a cheroot and flipped it into the street.

When she turned to go back into the saloon, she caught Bob's eye and smiled. It was *Ivy* the young prostitute. Bob acknowledged slightly and walked on with Boudine. "You know that Calico Queen there, Slye?"

"No."

A rather sad looking serving girl led them to a table in a plain but clean restaurant. "Will this do?" she uttered without expression.

"Yes, thank you," Bob replied, as he pulled out a chair for Boudine.

"We're out of the venison," the girl uttered in a near whisper, "but, we still got some hog and grits and steak and 'tater."

"Steak and 'taters for both of us," Bob said, as he sat opposite Boudine.

"And, two beers," Boudine ordered through her long bonnet. The serving girl turned and made her way through the partially filled room to the kitchen. Boudine leaned in toward Bob. "Feelin' better there, Bob?"

"What do you mean?"

"Well, a while back, you was already to skedaddle to who knows where and now you're here about to eat steak and 'taters with your new wife."

Bob leaned in closer to Boudine's long bonnet and hissed, "Will you stop that!"

"Guess all that rollin' around up in the room changed your mind there, Bob," she shot back with a chuckle.

The serving girl set the mugs of beer in front of them both and left.

"I still think we should make tracks and not stay

around here long. They'll be a posse and bounty hunters out after that reward, sure as hell."

"Well, that'd put us in a bad box if'n they catch us, won't it there, Bob..." Boudine loosened her long bonnet so she could sip her beer.

"You don't seem the bit perplexed about it, Boudine."

She leaned closer in, "It's just balderdash to get all slobbered up about gettin' caught, Slye, less'n they know who they're chasin' and they don't. Now, stop gettin' all fired up and simmer down. As far as anyone's business is concerned, we're on our way to Belle Fourche to homestead and that's it."

The serving girl brought their steaks and potatoes and set them on the table. "Anythin' else?" she asked softly.

"Keep the beers filled," Boudine answered with a tinge of callousness.

"Yes, ma'am," the girl mumbled and turned back toward the kitchen.

"You didn't have to be mean there, Boudine," Bob admonished.

Boudine sliced her thick steak. "Sometimes I get a terrible thirst after a good romp."

Two bearded men in well-worn, sweat-stained buckskins and coonskin caps entered and took the table nearest to Bob and Boudine. One of them leaned toward Bob as he set his rifle against the table and asked in a rather jovial way, "How's the grub here?"

"It'll do, sir. Steak and 'taters are passable."

The man replied, "Good. I been hankerin' for a good piece of steer meat for a long time."

"That'd be a Sharps Big Fifty there," Bob said indicating the man's rifle.

"Yessir, it is. Took us some buffalo on the way in to add to our pelts. You folks from around these parts?"

"No, sir. Just passin' through on our way to the Belle Fourche territory."

The man removed his coonskin cap and set it on the table. His face clouded a bit. So did his friend's. "Well, you might want to have another look at that thinkin', mister..."

"Bob Duncan and this is my wife... ah... Sally Mae."

The two men nodded to Boudine. "Name's Jonathan D'Amboise and this here's Nicholas Johansson."

The somber serving girl stepped to their table.

Jonathan ordered up, "Two steaks and 'taters for me."

"Same for me," Nicholas ordered nicely, "and whiskeys, if'n it ain't coffin varnish."

"Yessir," the serving girl muttered and left.

"You were sayin' about goin' to Belle Fourche, Mister D'Amboise," Bob asked.

"Yessir. We been trappin' the three rivers for near three months and just brought our pelts in to our buyer. And, not too soon. There's been some Lakota trouble thereabouts and south toward Fort Randall way we heard tell."

Bob shot Boudine a glance, then asked, "How much trouble, if I might ask?"

Nicholas Johansson added, "French trapper we

knew name of Fouquereau caught a Lakota arrow clear through the eye just a fortnight ago."

"Buried'im where we found'im," Jonathan added. "Was a good trapper too, he was."

The sad serving girl quietly delivered the two men their meals. "Your whiskeys will be comin'. Will there be anythin' else?"

Jonathan good-naturedly took her by her wrist and asked, "How much for you there?"

Without flinching, the serving girl answered in a dull, colorless voice, "That would be two dollars for one and five dollars for both at the same time."

The trapper's face blushed beneath his full beard. He let the girl's wrist slip away, as she turned back toward the kitchen. Nicholas heaved a sigh and sort of chuckled, "Well, I'll be hornswoggled..."

Back in the small hotel room, Bob paced. "That's the end of it; I'm off at first light. You can either come along or not. S'no nevermind to me."

Boudine sat on the edge of the bed, still in her dress. "I still think you be barkin' at a knot there, Slye. By the time you get to Fort Randall, all that mess will be mopped up."

NINE

Bob and Boudine were extra cautious heading south toward Fort Randall. It would be a full three days ride if the weather held true. The fall winds were dropping the nights to a chill and the snow flurries would not be far behind.

"I found me some extra loads back in Scooptown for the LaMat. One blast from that should set anyone off runnin'."

"Let's hope we don't need it."

It was moonless and pitch black out, when Bob whirled out of his bedroll and leveled his Peacemaker toward the woods that surrounded their encampment. Boudine was as quick as a rattler as she awoke from her catlike sleep and drew up the LaMat Grapeshot pistol and cocked the hammer. Neither said a word. Just listened and accustomed their eyes to the darkness. The campfire was just ash-covered coals.

The arrow that whistled by Boudine's ear, so close that she could feel the feathers, instantly set the LaMat in the direction from whence it came and exploded with a flash of fire and an earsplitting blast that echoed off into the distance. They both listened to the sounds of feet running away and then the clopping of the hooves of at least two or more horses beating a hasty retreat.

After a moment, Bob uttered, "Good thing..."

"What?" Boudine asked.

"You found the extra loads for the LaMat..."

The trail from Scooptown to Fort Randall was far from a hospitable one. It was not a well-traveled distance and wended through the South Dakota badlands. There were a few abandoned sod homesteads that showed the hazards of trying to put down roots in a hostile and unforgiving territory.

"No wonder you chose to become a bandit, Slye. Even the devil himself couldn't stand this place."

"It gets better, closer in toward the fort."

"Let's hope so. This's a godforsaken shithole..."

"Where'd you learn to cuss like you do, Boudine?"

"Calamity Jane."

"She must be quite somethin' to be around."

"Drink, cuss, shoot, fuck, that's her motto."

"Ladies cussin' ain't natural to me."

"I ain't a lady."

"And, men shouldn't cuss around a woman."

"Hell, you say, Slye! You cuss around me all the time."

"You ain't a woman... remember?"

The fall winds whipped in around them. Bob held up his hand to stop on a rise overlooking a more welcoming area with large crops of trees and a more fertile terrain coming into view. "Not far now. Half day at best."

Dusk was beginning to bring evening's blanket in and around the two riders. Bob dismounted and set the reins over the hitching post in front of the old sod schoolhouse where he had his early schooling. Something was different. Something was wrong. There was a pile of newly sawed beams off about twenty yards and the beginnings of what looked to be the start of a new building being erected. Bob saw the arrows sticking out of the sod wall and the broken down front door. He drew his Peacemaker and stepped forward. Boudine pulled her rifle from its scabbard and slipped quietly out of her saddle. Bob gave her a hand signal to go around the back.

At the door, Bob stopped and carefully looked inside. He cocked the hammer on his Peacemaker and waited until he was sure there was no movement. Boudine came around from the back side and shook her head. Bob pulled away the piece of the broken wooden door that was blocking his way and entered the schoolhouse. Boudine jerked one of the arrows out of the sod wall. "Lakota," she said, as she tossed it aside.

Inside, Bob found an oil lantern that hung on a peg. The same place it'd been when he was a schoolboy. He found the tin of matches next to it, lit the wick, and held the lantern up to illuminate the interior of the small room. The potbelly stove in the corner had been knocked sideways away from the black pipe smokestack that dangled down from the roof. He set the lantern on Miss Lundergan's desk table and picked up her overturned chair. Her teacher's books, papers and her big map book were scattered all over the wide board floor, along with the box of wooden words she had taught Bob to read and write with.

"This don't look good, Bob," Boudine said.

"No, it don't..."

"How far's your mother's homestead?"

"Spittin' distance."

"Let's go, then. Nothin' we can do here."

Bob and Boudine rode cautiously over the well-worn trail between his mother's homestead and the frontier school. There had not been much conflict with the Lakota, that Bob could remember, and the few homesteaders in the vicinity of Fort Randall. In fact, Millie Mae had traded with the Lakota tribe over the years and become friendly with several of the tribe members, inviting a few to take meals with her from time to time. However, what with the recent slaughter of Custer's troops at the *Battle of the Little Big Horn* and other U. S. Army excursions, as well as, the government's ongoing large land requisitions in the territory, things had changed and the clouds of conflict hung ominously over the South Dakota Territory.

Bob and Boudine sat quietly on their horses amongst a large clump of cottonwoods, just to the edge of Millie Mae's homestead. Not a sound. Not even a bird chirping. Millie Mae's dog Stubs did not come running and barking to greet them. The old workhorse and Dusty the mule were not to be seen. Nor were there any chickens pecking at the ground. Nor the goats. Nor the lambs that he knew his mother had added to her lot. Even her wagon was missing. Buzzer, the big fat mouser cat, who would have been waiting for handouts near the door at this hour was nowhere in sight.

Bob eased his roan forward. On the lookout. Ready. Boudine followed, drawing her rifle at the same time.

Bob signaled to stop several yards from the sod house where he was raised. He stepped down from his horse and drew the Winchester '73 from its scabbard. He handed the reins up to Boudine, then turned back to the house, heading quietly toward the front door.

It was nearing dark. Bob reached the front wall, then edged to the doorway with his Winchester set to fire. Boudine wrapped the roan's reins around her saddle horn and settled her rifle into her shoulder, steadying her aim at the doorway.

Bob stopped just at the doorframe for a moment. Listened intently, then silently started to turn his head, so's to see inside. Suddenly, without warning, something leapt out of the darkness from inside the house. Bob recoiled and flattened himself against the sod wall, just as a large gray blur skittered out and ran toward the bushes surrounding the spring-fed pond a distance away. He realized it was Buzzer, the big gray mouser, who had scooted out of the house. He glanced over at Boudine. She was still ready with her rifle. Steady as a post.

Bob again edged around the doorframe and slowly peered inside, waited, then stepped out in front of the open door, with his Winchester held waist high, aimed directly into the darkness.

Boudine watched intently. Bob slowly backed

away from the doorway, still holding his rifle ready to fire. He stopped about ten feet from the door and waited a moment. Then, a shadow appeared from inside. Someone came forward from within the dark interior. Boudine brought her rifle up to eye level and sighted in.

Just before coming into view, the shadowed form seemed to stumble and slump against the doorframe. Bob instantly held up his hand to Boudine, signaling her not to shoot.

What looked to be a middle-aged Indian woman faltered and started to fall forward. Bob quickly set his Winchester down and leapt to the doorway, grabbing her into his arms before she hit the ground. He then eased the Indian down onto her back.

Boudine spurred her horse closer, still keeping an eye out.

"Been shot. Help me get'im inside," Bob said to Boudine.

"You gonna try an' save her?"

"Friend of my mother's, name of Ogaleesha."

Inside the dark sod home, Bob and Boudine laid the wounded Indian onto the small bed that had been Bob's while growing up. Bob lit two lanterns that flared and spilled light into the room.

"See if you can get a fire goin' in the stove there and boil me some water."

"Don't look like much of a tussle went on here," Boudine said.

Bob pulled a chair next to the Indian. "The Bridesburg is gone."

"What?"

"My mother's '61 Army Bridesburg. Don't see it."

"Hell, that's an old single shot. She's out here with just a single shot?"

"Says it gives the animals a fightin' chance..."

Boudine stoked the fire in the potbelly stove. She then found some water in a pitcher, poured it into a small iron pot, and set it on the stove's cooking plate. Bob walked into the next room, holding the lantern out in front of him. There he saw that nothing seemed out of the ordinary. His plate daguerreotype photograph was in its folding black wood frame with the copper clasp, right next to his mother's bed where it should be. The bed was made up and the floor swept. The only thing different was the large unopened wooden shipping crate that held the window Bob had ordered back in Yankton and had shipped to her. Bob went to her sewing box on the small bureau and took out a spool wound with cotton thread and a sewing needle.

"Water's boilin'," Boudine told Bob, who was seated next the unconscious Indian.

"There should be some clean towels in that cupboard over the sink there," Bob said, indicating a two-shelved wooden cupboard attached to the wall over the washbasin. Boudine retrieved some hand-woven towels and brought them to him. Bob then gently undid the Indian's elaborately beaded belt with the hand-hammered ornate silver clasp. The gunshot wound, just below the rib cage, had soaked the Indian's faded red woven shirt and long skirt in blood. Bob gingerly pulled the shirt up over the Indian's chest to expose the extent of the wound. "Looks to be still in there," he uttered, "I'll have to get it out."

"That ain't no woman, Slye," Boudine announced with surprise, "that be a..."

"That's right. Over there in that chest, there should be a sharp skinnin' knife. Heat it in the water and bring it here."

Boudine quickly retrieved the knife and stuck the blade in the boiling water. "But, he's dressed like a woman there, Slye."

"Bring me the knife and the hot water and then you get ready to hold'im down when I start cuttin' out the bullet."

"You done this before?"

"Yes... lent a hand quite a few times over at the fort, when they were short of help after a battle."

Bob gently wiped away the oozing blood from the purplish-black wound and then started to extend the point of the skinning knife into the bullet hole. The Indian suddenly jerked in a spasm of pain. Boudine jumped forward and held his arms fast against the straw-filled mattress. Bob carefully continued. The Indian gritted his teeth and groaned, but did not resist Boudine...

It didn't take long for Bob to find the bullet. He carefully tipped it out of the wound and caught it in the palm of his hand; then he uttered, as he examined the slug, "Army issue..."

Outside, Bob mounted his horse under the light from a near full moon.

"How far's the fort?" Boudine asked, standing silhouetted in the doorway.

"'Bout five miles as the crow flies." Then he indicated, "Trail starts just yonder there. I want to find out if they know what happened here."

"What about the Injun?"

"Keep the wound clean and see if there's any food in the bin. Should be some 'taters and jerk around. You know any Lakota?"

"Some. Picked it up from the shows I did."

"See if he knows anything 'bout what happened here and keep an eye out. I shouldn't be too long. Any soldiers come 'round, don't let'em inside."

Bob reined the roan around in the direction of the trail.

"Be careful there, Slye." There was a wistfulness in Boudine's voice that Bob had not heard before. He tipped the brim of his *Boss of the Plains* hat and rode off at a quick pace.

The U.S. Army Private, one of two standing guard in the semi-darkness at the main gate of Fort Randall, held his rifle at the ready as Bob approached. "Hold up there!" he ordered.

Bob slowed his horse to a walk and held up his free hand. "The name's Robert Duncan from yonder homestead. Be looking to see if Master Sergeant Bartholomew is about."

The young private's stern voice belied his youth, "What is the nature of your business, sir?"

"My mother's homestead was attacked and she and all her animals are missing. Her name is Millie Mae

Duncan. She trades here with the cook, Jasper Spence, and is a friend of Sergeant Bartholomew."

The young private studied Bob for a moment, and then nodded to the second soldier who shoved open one half of the log gate. "I believe she's been quartered next to the main headquarters building. It's back toward the..."

"I know where it is, thank you, Private," Bob said and guided his horse through the gate into the fort.

"How is it he dresses like a woman there, Slye?"

"Two Spirits, they're known as. Winkté, by the Lakota."

"So's they dresses like a woman an' they're really a man then."

"He's a mystic and a healer."

"I ain't never heard of it put that way."

"They revere them as spiritual. He's been an acquaintance of my mother's for a time."

"I've got to think about this a bit..."

The private knocked on the door of a small lodging cabin next to the Army Headquarters building. Bob then heard his mother's voice, "Yes?"

"It's Private Dolan, ma'am, I have someone here to see you."

The sound of the door latch could be heard. The door opened slowly. Bob was standing just behind the private, but was a head taller. Millie Mae immediately recognized her son. Her strong, tanned, weathered face became a vision of pure joy. She pulled the door open wide. The private stepped to the side. Millie Mae reached up and wrapped her arms around Bob's neck, knocking his *Boss of the Plains* hat to the wooden plank porch. She whispered to him, "I felt you comin', Son. I felt you comin'."

Bob sat at a small table opposite his mother in the spotless army cabin, with a warm fire crackling in the fireplace. An oil lamp flickered over their faces. "There's that Lakota mystic, Ogaleesha, layin' wounded at the homestead. I got the bullet out and stitched him as best I could."

"They're going to take me and the animals back tomorrow. Mister Bartholomew is out runnin' down the last of the renegades and sent word that we were allowed to return. But, don't say nothin' about Ogaleesha. Might not be safe for him yet."

"I saw, comin' in, that the school was attacked and Miss Lundergan was nowhere about."

"They think she was taken. They be lookin' for her. Just pray, Son, just pray."

Private Dolan and another private escorted Millie Mae as she drove her buckboard, loaded up with two branch-woven chicken cages, four goats and two lambs. Dusty the mule and a new milk cow trotted along behind attached by lengths of rope. Stubs the dog ran ahead of Bob on the trail. Bob held up his hand a distance away from the homestead that appeared on the horizon. The party stopped. Bob reined his horse around in the direction of the two army escorts. "I can take it from here, gentlemen."

"Are you sure, sir?" asked Private Dolan.

"Very sure. I thank you for your kindness and for taking good care of my mother. It is very much appreciated."

"Then we'll be off, sir." Private Dolan offered, "Sergeant Bartholomew informed me that he will be out to check on things as soon as he's back from his mission." With that, the two soldiers turned back and rode off along the trail.

"Mister Bartholomew came for us and moved us to the fort because of the disturbance. We were never in danger..."

"There's a travelin' companion at the homestead tendin' to Ogaleesha."

"I look forward to meeting him."

"S'not a him... 'tis a her."

"A woman?"

"More of a cowboy than a woman..."

When they were nearing the homestead, Bob noticed that Boudine was off bathing in the spring-fed pond and was standing ankle deep in all that nature intended. He let out a loud whistle and Boudine responded by hurrying to get out of the water and pull on her clothes. "That be Sally Mae Boudine," Bob said to his mother.

As Millie Mae stepped down off the buckboard, Boudine came striding up the path from the pond, all smiles and fresh as a daisy. She reached Millie Mae and stuck out her hand. "I'm Sally Mae Boudine, ma'am. You must be Bob's mother that he's forever talkin' about," she said brightly, as she grasped Millie Mae's hand and shook it firmly. "I took the opportunity to wash out the towels we used on your Injun friend in there. Hung'em out to dry on yonder line," she said, indicating the rope with the clothes drying on the line that extended from the corner of the sod house to a pole in the ground. "Also washed out his shirt there, so's he'll have it to travel with when he's ready."

Millie Mae stood there trying to take in this whirlwind she had just met.

Boudine continued with her rapid-fire account of what went on while Bob was at the fort. "Found your root cellar over yonder and boiled up some 'taters, turnips, carrots and the hare I shot, into a soup that seemed to help'im. Also, kept the wound cleaned out, but he could use some medicine, I suspect. Didn't know where to look for that."

Millie Mae attempted to utter, "Ah... thank you... Miss..."

"Sally Mae, ma'am. But, Bob here just calls me Boudine. Boudine is fine."

Millie Mae glanced at Bob, who was wrapping his horse's reins around the hitching post. "I think Sally Mae will do. Nice to meet you."

Millie Mae untied the mule and the milk cow, letting them wander down to the pond, and let down the rear gate of the wagon so the lambs and goats could jump out. She then headed for the open front door of the house. "Bob, if'n you could unhitch the horse and empty the chicken cages that'd help." To Boudine she said, "You come with me, Sally Mae, and we'll see what we've got goin' here."

Bob watched all of this with a bit of dismay

coming over him. His mother was never one to take to anyone on first look, especially someone the likes of Sally Mae Boudine. He also became aware that, as Boudine ran her hands through her clean brown hair and shook the water loose, she had let her hair grow longer than he had ever noticed and that she somehow seemed more of a woman than before.

Inside the sod house, Millie Mae sat in a ladder-back chair by the bed and examined Ogaleesha's wound that Boudine had covered with a clean cloth folded into a pad. "That looks to heal up nice, if'n the infection stays away." She indicated a small wooden chest of drawers against the wall. "There's a tin of yarrow grind in there. Take some and mix it with water in a cup and make me up a paste."

Boudine retrieved the tin and did exactly as she was asked, then brought it to her. Millie Mae scooped the yarrow paste out of the cup and proceeded to gently press an amount into and around the wound. "This stops the bleedin' and starts the cure," Millie Mae explained.

Boudine watched with interest, then added, "He said 't'was soldiers who shot'im yesterday. Said he was headed to see if you were here, so's he could warn you. Said he was able to hide out until they went on their way."

"You speak Lakota?" Millie Mae inquired.

"A fair amount."

Just then, Bob entered. "How's it look?"

"You done a fair job, Son. He's lucky y'all were here."

"Looked to be not too deep. Was stopped by the rib bone."

Ogaleesha tried to sit up. Millie Mae put her hand firmly on his shoulder and stopped him. He laid back down.

Boudine stood up, "I have to use the privy." She brushed by Bob and left the house.

Millie Mae turned in her chair, "That be quite a woman you got yourself there, Bob."

"I don't got myself anything there, Mother. She's just a friend."

Millie Mae paused knowingly, "I see..."

"Just a friend, Mother, just a friend... Like you say about you and Sergeant Bartholomew..."

Millie Mae tried to hide the slight smile that started at the corners of her mouth by turning her head away from Bob, "I see..."

"I want to thank you for sending the window, Son. That was a most generous surprise."

"I always said I was going to get you more light in here, Mother, remember?"

"I do, I certainly do... It was quite expensive, was it not?"

"Not as much as you think."

"Still and all... to send it all the way from Yankton. Must be hundreds of miles as the crow flies."

"Don't fret. Just as long as it got here."

"I wasn't going to ask, but a mother's curiosity does catch up once in a while. Especially, when it comes to her own..."

"What is it, then?"

"What exactly is it that you do for work nowadays, Robert?"

"Well, I've been quite fortunate of late, especially over in Deadwood where all the gold mining is going on."

"I see... and it's the mining for gold that you do?"

"In a matter of speaking... yes... I search for gold."

"And, the girl... she mines for gold as well?"

"Not exactly... She's a sharpshooter in a Wild West Show..."

"Wild West Show? I don't believe I... I don't understand."

"I'll let her explain it to you, Mother..."

"She likes you, y'know..."

"No, she don't."

"Oh, yes... I see her lookin' at you with that look in her eyes."

"Believe me, Mother; she likes me 'bout as much as a rattlesnake likes a mongoose..."

Three ladder-back chairs had been set outside the sod house and a lighted lantern set on the ground. The night was clear and the heavens above were awash with millions of bright twinkling stars. The three sat there quietly. Bob smoked one of his cheroots, as did Boudine.

"That was a fine meal you served up there, Missus Duncan."

"Millie Mae," she said to Boudine, as she stroked Stubs head beside her.

"Yes, ma'am," Boudine said.

"It wouldn't have been much, hadn't been for those fine quail you brought in," Millie Mae said.

Bob knocked an ash from his cheroot onto the ground. Boudine looked up at the stars. "I can see why you like livin' here. It's really purdy."

"It ain't so 'purdy' in the winter or the scorchin' summer, Boudine," Bob offered.

"Sally Mae," Millie Mae corrected.

"Mmmm..." was Bob's reply, then he added, "It's too dangerous out here alone, what with the Sioux risin' up."

"I ain't alone. I got Mister Bartholomew comin' round and 'sides, the Lakota and I have always gotten along with our respect for each other. Ogaleesha be in there because he knew I would welcome him and be able to help."

"Well, be that as it may, I have a plan brewin'," Bob said.

"What kind of plan is that, Son?" Millie Mae asked skeptically.

"Shhhh!" Boudine uttered and held up her hand. She squinted at the darkness toward a rise in the land with the night's gray glow rising up behind it. She then, slowly reached for her pistol that was in its holster looped over the chair back. She drew it out and aimed it toward the rise. Both Bob and Millie Mae looked in the direction she was aiming.

Millie Mae eased her hand out toward Boudine and quietly said, "Holster that, Sally Mae, you won't be needin' it."

Barely able to be seen were the silhouettes of two Indian riders on horseback standing stalk-still. Waiting. A third silhouette was of a horse with a travois pull hitched behind it. Millie stood and slowly advanced toward the riders. She signaled them forward. "They've come for Ogaleesha," she said calmly.

"How'd they know he was here?" Boudine asked.

"They know..." Millie Mae answered softly.

"You little sumbitch! I'll teach you to backtalk at me." With that, Jessup Slye jerked the thick leather belt out his wool pant loops and drunkenly reached out for young Bob Slye, as he cowered in the corner of the sod house.

"Stop!" shouted his young mother, Millie Mae Slye. Jessup whipped back his fist and backhanded her right across her cheek, sending her crashing into the table and down onto the dirt floor, stunned from the vicious blow. He then reached out, grabbed Bob by the hair, and dragged the youngster outside. "Take them britches off!"

"No!" Bob cried out.

"Oh, 'No' is it? I'll show you, Little Slye!" With that, Jessup started beating Bob with the belt with abandon, hitting him wherever the leather would land.

Out of breath, with spittle spraying from his mouth, Jessup shouted, "This'll be a beatin' you'll never forget, you little shite!"

Again and again, the thick leather belt laid into Bob's skinny body, until suddenly there was the crash of the chair that Millie Mae brought down onto Jessup's head and back. Jessup stopped, stood up and tried to focus on what had happened. His eyes rolled up into his head and his body fell limp, like a horse that had just been shot.

"That ain't ever going to happen to you again, Son... Never..."

The morning sun spilled over the prairie. The three chairs were no longer outside the sod house. Millie Mae was already letting the chickens out of their coop and tossing scratch over the ground. She then headed to the small corral and the sod and wood built shed and let the animals out to graze. The goats and the lambs scampered about and the milk cow, workhorse and Dusty the mule, headed down to the pond to quench their morning thirst.

Stubs ran to Bob as he came outside still in his undergarments and pants. He picked up a bucket by the door and walked toward the coop.

"Eggs?"

"Two days' worth."

"I'll fetch'em."

Over breakfast of eggs, potatoes and coffee, Bob again broached the subject of his concern for Millie Mae. "You could spend the rest of your life scratchin' at this patch of land and never have it amount to much more than a dust pile in the end. There're other places north of here that are much more partial to farming, hunting and fishing that would suit you better, if'n that's what you're of a mind to do. And, from what I hear, the ones who are settlin' there will be growin' supplies for the new homesteaders and miners that're headin' their way.

Boudine was silent, as Millie smiled and leaned over her plate toward Bob. "This is my land. I proved it up according to the government. No one can take it away."

"But, that could be the same for another homestead with better land to prove up on."

"Have you seen this land for yourself, Robert?" Millie Mae pressed.

Bob hesitated, "No... not exactly."

Millie Mae leaned back in her chair. "Well, then, it's a bird in the hand I'd say..."

The target Boudine had set up was made of two branches tied together in a cross, with the shorter one shoulder high and the longer one stabbed into the soft ground just up from the pond. She stood next to Millie Mae about the length of four covered wagons from the target. "Now think of that as a gunslinger who's about to draw on'ya," she instructed. Bob sat in a chair outside the sod house, a distance away, making notes in his leather-wrapped notebook.

"Alright," Millie Mae said quietly, but intrigued nonetheless.

With a draw that was faster than a lightning burst, Boudine drew her pistol and fanned off her 'King-Queen-Ace' shots that blasted the tips off the ends of the short pole and the top of the longer one. She then twirled the pistol and smoothly holstered it. "'That's one of the acts I do in the Wild West Show," she explained with a sense of pride. "It's called the 'King-Queen-Ace' with the Ace bein' the gunslinger's head. 'Cept in the show they have a target dressed up like a gunslinger, not a real one."

"I didn't think so. That's some pretty good shootin' there, Sally Mae. And, folks pay good money to see that, do they?"

"Oh, there's more than just that, ma'am. There's all kinds of shootin' and ridin' and stampedes and Injun raids and the likes."

"Well, I wouldn't know about that. The news comes pretty slow hereabouts. Mostly, from when I visit the fort or when Mister Bartholomew comes on over."

They started back toward the house, as Stubs ran

over to the busted up stick target and sniffed all around. "Will you be doin' more of those shows, Sally Mae?"

"Don't know. I'll have to see how things have changed since ol' Wild Bill Hickok was kilt."

"I believe I did hear about that from Jasper Spence, the cook at the fort, when I delivered him some 'taters and turnips 'bout a fortnight ago."

"Yup, got himself bushwhacked by a drunkin' gambler whilst playin' poker in Deadwood."

"Well, if'n you play in the devil's playground, you're bound to get burned by the hellfire," Millie Mae said, as they approached Bob, who was wrapping up his notebook in its leather cover.

"Bob was there the day it happened, weren't you, Bob?" Boudine said to Bob with a bit of a challenging grin.

"What was that?" Bob answered.

"She says you was there when Wild Bill Hickok was killed," Millie Mae interjected.

Bob stood up and inserted his Eberhard lead pencil into the leather tie around his notebook. "I wasn't there," he said firmly with a sharp look at Boudine, "I heard the shot as I was ridin' out of town. Didn't know it was him 'til I saw it in a newspaper days later over in Scooptown."

Millie Mae put an end to it, "Well, no matter. 'The Lord's Will' I always say." Then, she asked Bob, "What're you writin' there, Son?"

"Just some reminders. Nothin' special..."

"He's always jottin' down somethin' in that notebook of his. Won't tell anyone what's in it," Boudine said.

"Well, he was always good at writin' and readin' when he was at the schoolhouse. Fact is, he was Miss Lundergan's favorite, weren't you, Bob?"

Bob felt a redness come to his face and turned and took the chair up by its ladder back and headed for the sod house doorway. "So you say, Mother," he uttered. He stopped, when Boudine warned, "Rider comin', yonder..."

Master Sergeant William Harrison Bartholomew rode in over the expanse, quickly dismounted and wrapped his horse's reins around the hitching post. Although, he looked to have been out on a mission for quite some time, he was a robust man in his full Army battlefield uniform, with a full mustache and beard, who looked to be in his early forties, as was Millie Mae. He went right to Bob, shook his hand and grasped him by his shoulders. "My goodness, Bob! Just look at you. You must've grown a foot since I last saw you," Bartholomew expressed with a wide grin.

"I believe you're exaggeratin' a bit there, Master Sergeant," replied Bob.

"Bill... to you there, Bob."

"Yessir."

"And, who do we have here then?" Bartholomew asked, referring to Boudine.

Boudine quickly reached her hand out to Bartholomew, "Sally Mae Boudine."

The Sergeant apprehensively shook Boudine's hand while giving her a quick up and down study.

"Should I brew up some Arbuckle's?" Millie Mae asked, obviously happy that Bartholomew had arrived,

"You look like you ain't had much sleep by your appearance."

He held up his hand, "Thank you, Millie, but this is just a quick visit. I have to get back to my troops. They're at the fort gettin' fortified and ready to go out again. His voice took on a more official tone. "I came here for two reasons. I wanted to make sure you arrived back here safe and sound and, by the look of things, you have done just that. And, I wanted to tell you so you could spread the word amongst the other homesteaders, that this area has been cleared of Lakota. The Black Hills have been taken by the United States Government with the signing of the Indian Appropriations Act of 1876, which means all of the Sioux must disperse the Hills and retreat to their reservations."

"My-my..." uttered Millie Mae, with a sense of foreboding.

"Doesn't mean there won't be some renegades who refuse to give up, but the thinkin' from Washington is that this war will be finished sometime in '77, the good Lord willin'."

"Your horse could use a waterin' I suspect," offered Bob.

"Yes, you tag along with me, Bob, I have somethin' to discuss." With that, Bartholomew took his horse's reins and headed toward the pond with Bob right along with him, leaving the two women to wonder.

At the water's edge the horse drank down its thirst. Bartholomew turned to Bob. "Tell me, Bob, how've you been keepin'?"

"Well, I'm not the worse for wear, I feel."

"Good-good... Good to hear..." There was an obvious apprehensiveness in the sergeant's tone. "And, you've found work in your travels?"

"Yessir..."

"Good-good... Good to hear..." Then, Bartholomew asked, "And, your woman there, she's..."

Bob interrupted, "She's not my woman. Just travelin' together. Two's better'n one nowadays."

"Yes... right... And, she's found work along the way, has she?"

"Yessir, she's a sharpshooter with the Wild West Show."

"Oh, is that right?" Bartholomew said, a bit surprised, then a thought triggered in his head, "She wouldn't have traveled the one with Wild Bill Hickok and Calamity Jane now, would she?"

"I believe that's the one, sir."

Bartholomew pushed his uniform hat back and scratched his head. "Well, I'll be hornswoggled. I believe Wild Bill told me about a young sharpshooter who was a woman who dressed up like a boy in the show, when he hired on to guard a gold shipment to the fort a year back. She that one?"

"Yessir, I believe she be the one," Bob answered a bit uneasily. Stubs ran up and sniffed happily at the sergeant, who crouched down and patted the tail-wagging dog.

"Well, that's somethin', ain't it?... That's really somethin'," he said with a bit of a troubled sigh. He stood back up and paused to look out over the pond and the lands to the horizon. After a moment, he asked, "So, just what is it you do for a livin' now, Bob?"

Bob knew the question was meaningful. He tried to force down the dryness rising in his throat. "I tried cowboyin' for a while and then worked the Wichita yards killin' steers." He stopped there and waited.

"And, now, Bob? What about now?" Bartholomew pressed, "What is it you do for work now?"

Bob looked down at the ground and then over toward his mother, who was standing talking with Boudine near the sod house door. Master Sergeant Bartholomew had been a friend of his mother's since Bob was near fourteen and had, most certainly, been an influence in his life. Where his mother concentrated on the teachings of the Bible and making sure that Bob was able to get enough book learning before he set out on his own, Bartholomew filled in a worldlier void, as did his card playing tutelage under the watchful eye of the fort's cook, Jasper Spence. He owed Bartholomew a lot. He owed him the truth... Some truth...

After a pause, Bob replied, "I play cards."

"I see," said Bartholomew, with a glance in Millie Mae's direction. "Might not be something to discuss with your mother." Bob nodded his agreement. "Are you good at gambling then?" Bartholomew continued.

"It has been an agreeable enterprise," Bob replied.

"Guess we have that old biscuit-puller Jasper to thank for that," Bartholomew said, with a bit of a chuckle. Then, he added, "So, that be the sum'n'substance of it then? Just gambling?" There was an undercurrent in the sergeant's question that made Bob uneasy.

"Well, everything's a gamble nowadays," Bob answered guardedly.

Bartholomew studied Bob. "Yes, it is... Indeed it is?" Then he continued without waiting for a comment from Bob, "Ever gambled out there in Deadwood?"

"Yessir..."

"Old Wild Bill told me t'was his favorite place to sit down for a poker game. Guess he made a living out of it, so he said. Ever meet up with'im there in Deadwood, Bob?"

Bob chose his words carefully, "Matter of fact, I did. Night before he was bushwhacked. Played against him and some of his friends."

"Really... How'd you do?"

"Won mostly," Bob answered.

"Were you there when he was shot?"

"Nossir, but I come to find out the shot I heard when I was ridin' out of town was the one that killed him."

"You don't say... Ever gamble over in Scooptown?"

Now, Bob knew he had to be very careful about what he said. "Some..."

"I hear the gambling over there in Yankton is a bit quieter and fancier than Deadwood and Scooptown."

"A bit," Bob replied.

"Almost had to add a detachment from our fort to go with Custer's to Little Big Horn. Lucky for us, they didn't carry out the order."

"We saw Custer comin' through Yankton on his way," Bob said, as he watched Bartholomew's eyes for a sign of where the conversation was headed.

"We?"

This took Bob off guard, but he replied with, "Boudine there was travelin' with me at the time."

"I see..." The sergeant paused then asked, "Are you married to that gal, Bob?"

Bob felt his stomach jump at the question, "Nossir! No, I am not." His voice was louder than he had intended. The sergeant raised his hand and smiled.

"Easy, I was just asking that's all. If she's not the one, then it's none of my business." Bartholomew's horse snorted and raised its head up from the water. The sergeant took the reins and started leading the mount away from the pond in the opposite direction of the house.

"Come on, don't want him pissing in the pond. Your mother gets all up and about with that," Bartholomew chuckled.

As they strolled away from the pond, the sergeant took on a more serious tone, "Bob, I have something to tell you..."

"Yessir?"

"Well, for a long time, I know your mother has told you that we are just friends... Well, I have to tell you that it's grown to be much more than that."

Bob breathed in and out and said, "I suspected..."

"For how long?"

"For quite some years, I felt you both had a liking for each other."

The horse stopped and began to relieve itself. The two men stepped further in front, so's not to be splashed.

"Do you approve then, Bob?" Bartholomew

asked.

Bob looked at the sergeant, glad that his questioning might be over, then answered, "I think it is fine that you both have someone to care for each other."

Bartholomew heaved a sigh, "Well, that's settled then. I wanted to say something to you; because I'm sure Millie Mae would not. Also, I'll be mustering out of the Army come a year from now and we've decided to stay together, as your mother says, 'Under God's watch'. Would that suit you, Bob?"

"Yessir. That would be fine with me."

The horse spotted some tufts of grass and started to graze. Bartholomew dropped the reins and turned to Bob. "She a gambler too, Bob?" The question threw Bob. "Your woman friend, is she a poker player?"

Bob tried not to show his surprise at the sudden question. "She does play cards from time to time..."

"How do those gamblers there in Deadwood like playing their hand to a woman at the table?"

Bob's throat went dry and he coughed. Then answered with, "I've never played at a table with her..."

Bartholomew said, "Oh, I forgot, she used to travel in the Wild West Show posing as a boy, right?"

"So I've been told..."

"And, you're sure you're not married there, Bob?"

Bob gritted back his feelings and looked away without answering. Bartholomew then uttered, "I guess I already asked you that..." There was an awkward pause. Then, Bartholomew reached into his uniform shirt and brought out a folded piece of paper. "Bob... did you know that there might be someone out there using your name?"

Bob looked back at Bartholomew, "Sir?"

Bartholomew opened the folded rumpled paper and handed it to Bob. It was the wanted poster that Bob first saw early on before one of his stage robberies; the one that was first held up by Boudine in advance. Bob looked at the poster and handed it back to the sergeant. "I know about this. Tore one off of a tree quite some time back."

"Says, the 'Bandit Bob Slye' there, Bob," Bartholomew offered with a bit of trepidation.

"Haven't used that name ever since Jessup took his leave."

"I know that, Bob. I surely do. But, it seems a coincidence here that you were about during the time of some of these robberies. Also, a train robbery over in Yankton with two bandits on that one. About the time Custer came through on his way to Little Big Horn there, Bob..."

"Where would they get the name of 'Bob Slye' anyway?" Bob asked, a tad defensively.

"Don't rightly know there, Bob... Seems a puzzlement..."

Bob began to harden, "I'm not sure what you're drivin' at here, Sergeant."

"I'm just asking, Bob... Have you ever killed anyone? We get requests from time to time from the civilian law to keep an eye out, that's all..." He looked at Bob for a reaction. There was none, other than to say, "No, I've not killed anyone."

Bartholomew considered this, then changed the subject. "With you bein' so far away, would there be a place to send you a letter, should your mother have a need to? She has a mother's worries from time to time."

Bob thought about this for a moment then said, "There's the Wells Fargo Office there in Deadwood. Might be a place."

Bartholomew pondered that, as he walked over and picked up his horse's reins. "I better be gettin' back to the fort. My company will be headin' out again 'fore nightfall."

They started back toward the house. Bartholomew asked, "Where're you headed next then, Bob?"

"Toward Belle Fourche territory, I'm thinkin'."

"Belle Fourche-Belle Fourche," Bartholomew repeated. "Good fishing and hunting in those parts. Don't think there'll be many gambling halls for you, Bob."

"Thinkin' about lookin' to homestead thereabouts and then convincin' my mother to leave here and prove up a producing farm. Might be a better place for you both. Folks movin' this way from all over and they're going to need supplies of food. Lots of good plantin' land there, I've been told. Maybe, set up a trading post, as well."

"Well, that's a pretty tall order. Be a much better situation, if that be the case. Hope you've saved your winnings there, Bob?"

Bob paused, then answered, "I have, sir... I have..."

"Girl going with you?"

"Don't know. Can't imagine it..."

"Well, you two men solved everyone's problems there?" Millie Mae said happily, as Bob and Sergeant Bartholomew approached.

Bartholomew covered with a hearty laugh, "We surely did, there Millie Mae, we surely did. Didn't we, Bob."

"Yep..."

"Oh, I almost forgot," Bartholomew announced, "Your old teacher, Miss Lundergan, has been found alive and well. Seems, one of her older boy students stayed behind to help her out after school and was able to get her out of there just before the school was raided. Hid in the hills and turned up at the fort early this morning."

"Oh, that's wonderful," Millie Mae said, looking to the heavens. "Praise the Lord! Isn't that good news, Bob? "

"...Yes, it is," Bob uttered, almost under his breath.

The sergeant mounted up. "Millie Mae, you keep a watch out, hear? I know you have good relations with the Lakota, but a word to the wise. I'll be back around soon as I return." Then to Bob, he said pointedly, "You be careful there, son. Sometimes it's good to gather in the harvest before it starts rotting in the field." He brought his horse closer to Boudine and tipped his hat, "Nice to meet you, ma'am. Maybe someday you can show me your shooting tricks." With that, Master Sergeant Bartholomew reined his horse around and rode away back toward Fort Randall. Stubs sprinted after them. Caught up. Passed them. Then stopped, having won the race.

"How the hell d'he know I was in the Wild West Show?"
"Hickok told'im."
"Hickok? How'd he come by Wild Bill?"
"Met'im when he guarded a gold shipment to the fort..."
"Damn! He say anythin' else?"
"Not about you..."
"'Bout you, then?"
"Some."
"Some what?"
"Asked if we was married..."

Bob finished setting the new front window into the widened opening he had cut into the sod wall next to the front door. As he grabbed up a handful of straw mixed with mud from a wooden bucket and started stuffing it into the spaces around the new window, two shots cracked the quiet out on the prairie. The late afternoon sun dropped further down toward the horizon.

"That's either two birds or two rabbits for dinner," Bob called over to his mother.

"How do you know it'll be two?" Millie Mae asked, as she led Dusty the mule and the milk cow into the small corral with the goats and lambs, just off the animal shed, and shut the gate.

"She never misses."

Millie Mae picked up her milk pail and headed for the sod house. "'Taters, turnips or boiled corn? I'll get some water heated up."

Bob said, "Mother..."

"Yes, Son?"

Bob waited until she was closer and stopped

working on the window. "I would hope that you might at least do some thinkin' on the subject of possibly relocatin', if I'm able to find a more suitable place for a real producing farm. I plan to go up to Belle Fourche territory where the three rivers come together and have a look-see."

Millie Mae went quiet until she reached the doorway and was met by Buzzer the cat, who sidled up to Millie's leg with a rub, knowing there would be some milk as a reward. She knelt down, picked up the gray mouser, and patted it. "Son," she began thoughtfully, "...this is where I live. It's mine and yours when the day comes and it's paid for itself along the way. Ever since back before, I vowed, with God's help, to be able to care for myself and to care for you, the best way I know how. Sometimes, it has been a struggle, I admit that..." She set the cat down and continued, "But, I know this land and it knows me and..."

Bob interrupted, "Mother, there's the Indian Wars goin' on all around here on up to the Black Hills. Sergeant Bartholomew says that it looks to be another year before they'll be an end to it."

"The Lakota and I understand each other. We have no quarrel. They have a bickerin' with the United States Government that they are going to settle come the day, and we will go on as we were. That's why Ogaleesha know'd to come here and why his people know'd where to find him. It's God's way and it's my way..." With that, Millie Mae entered the house, leaving Bob to stand where he was.

"The sergeant had that wanted poster with my name on

it."

"Your name?"
"The name of 'Slye'."
"It is your name there, Slye."
"No, it ain't! It's Duncan, dammit!
"...Well, it is a puzzlement, there Duncan-Dammit."
"Yes... it is a puzzlement."

"I wish you could stay on a bit, Son," Millie Mae said as she watched Boudine rein her horse around and swing up into the saddle in a smooth mount.

Bob held the reins to the roan, stepped over to his mother, and kissed her lightly on her cheek. The sun was just breaking over the horizon and there was a fall crisp in the air. The horses snorted steam, as they anticipated the next journey and pawed at the earth. Bob stepped a foot into the stirrup and set himself into the saddle. "I still would appreciate it if'n you could tell me you would think about what I said..."

Millie Mae smiled a bit and said, "You know, I always think on the things you say. Now, you should be on your way. I smell the flurries comin'."

Bob looked out across the prairie, touched his fingers to the brim of his *Boss of the Plains* hat, turned his horse and rode off at a steady gait. Boudine nodded to Millie Mae and followed right along beside Bob. Stubs did not run after the two, but chose to sit next to Millie Mae as she watched after them.

HANGIN' WITH THE TRUTH

TEN

"Your Ma is a strong one..."
"She is... She is that."
"She say anythin' 'bout me?"
"Just what mothers ask."
"What?"
"Nothin' special."
"She ask if I was with you?"
"Wasn't like that."
"Like what then?"
"She asked me if the good Lord would be happy about us being together..."
"Damn... She really ask that?"
"Yes..."
"Well then, Slye, d'you think he is?"
"You'll have to ask him yourself..."

The ride north into Belle Fourche territory was pretty much a hit or miss venture as far as trails went. There were hunting trails the Lakota and trappers used, but they did not head in any particular direction. There were buffalo migrating trails across the plains that only led to where the herds roamed. Homesteads did not begin to appear until they were closer to where the Belle Fourche, Redwater River and Hay Creek converged. But, first, Bob and Boudine had to traverse through miles of open rocky land that turned into rugged canyons and gorges, testing their endurance to the hilt. "This ain't goin' along with my way of thinkin' there, Bob. 'T'aint at all what I'm thinkin'."

"We have a ways to go yet, Boudine."

"Give me a card game or a full-up Wells Fargo Stage to take and I'll be happy."

The closer they came to where the Belle Fourche converged with the other waterways, the more fertile the hills and open land became. Clusters of trees became thick woods. Game of all kinds thrived. As they rode on, they found that the new farmers were not settled close together. They were sparse and quite far apart. They went about proving up their farmlands or homesteads and, in some instances, just building on where they happened to feel was a good plot of land to settle; since there did not seem to be any sort of strict government regulation or plan thereabouts. Nor were there any obvious boundaries that existed. The only objections appeared to come from some of the Sioux tribes, who were already established in the Belle Fourche territory, long before the white man's intrusion.

Bob sat on his mount and let his horse drink from the clear, flowing river in front of him. Boudine dismounted and let her horse drink its thirst down. They had arrived at where the rivers met.

As dusk settled in, Bob set out his bedroll and

saddle next to the flickering campfire. A rather large dressed-out jackrabbit, nearly as big as Stubs the dog, roasted on a spit made of sticks over the flames. Boudine was seated on the ground nearby rummaging, rather agitatedly, through her saddlebags. "What're you lookin' for there, Boudine?"

"Nothin'," she uttered sharply.

Bob turned the spit around so the rabbit would cook on the other side. "Well, nothin' must be somethin'. Noticed you been lookin' through them bags of yours and actin' ratty near everytime we stopped."

She threw the bags off in a heap. "S'nothin', I said."

"You lose somethin' then?"

Boudine didn't answer.

Bob straightened up, reached into his pants pocket and came up with a fist-sized leather pouch tied with rawhide at the top. He dangled it out of reach of Boudine. "Lookin' for this, Boudine?"

A look of intense surprise and anger flashed over Boudine's face. "Where the hell d'you find that?" she burst out, as she jumped up and tried to grab at the pouch. Bob whipped it away. "Gimme that!" Bob held it up over his head. Boudine flailed at it, trying to grab it away. "That's mine, goddammit! Gimme that or else!"

"Or else what?"

"Or else I'll cut your sack off and throw it in the fire."

"I believe you're serious..."

"Goddamned right I'm serious."

Bob tossed the pouch onto the ground. Boudine immediately retrieved it. "Where the hell d'you find it?"

"You left it in the privy back at the homestead."

"Shit! You could'a said somethin', Slye... Shit!"

"What is it?"

"None of your stinkin' business," she mutterd, as if caught at something.

"That what you were after over there in Scooptown, when you went over t'the Chinese part of town?"

Boudine glared at Bob. "I said, it's none of your goddamned business." She then walked off into the darkness toward the river.

"Where're you goin'?"

"Do what I have to do," came the answer from the shadows...

The fire had turned to glowing embers. The rabbit was no longer on the spit. Both Bob and Boudine were wrapped up in their separate bedrolls. Crickets chirped. The moonlight filtered down through the overhanging trees and cast glancing reflections off the flowing ripples on the river.

"Slye?" came Boudine's low voice.

"Mmm?"

"You don't know much 'bout women, do ya?"

"Know s'much as I need, I reckon."

"That says you don't know much."

"What're you gettin' to there?"

"Tell'ya come daylight..."

Daylight came with a pale gray frost painted over the grass and fallen leaves from the trees. The rising sun would soon disperse the hint of fall. The fire was out and the ashes scratched away. Bob took a chew of jerky and wrapped the rest in a piece of oilcloth, then put it back into his saddlebag. He checked the saddle's cinch and tightened it up. Boudine came out from behind some nearby bushes, wiping her nose on her sleeve as she mounted up. "Still don't know why you want to get started so early," she said to Bob.

Bob stepped into the stirrup and swung into the saddle. "Want to see if there's any homesteaders up and about who I might speak with."

"Chinese medicine..." Boudine said, breaking the silence, as the two rode along the riverbank.

"What?"

"That's what's in the pouch... Chinese medicine."

"Oh..." Bob uttered.

"It's for the tireds," Boudine said.

Bob shoved back a low hanging tree branch that was about to slap him in the face and held it back for Boudine to pass. "What is it?" he asked, as they continued on.

"Don't know, but it works wonders."

"I see..."

"And, for the *curse...*"

Bob hesitated then asked, quite confused, "The what?"

"See, I told you. Ya-don't know nothin' about women."

"What's a curse? Like a witch doctor or somethin'?"

"Shit-damn, Slye! Didn't your Ma never tell you 'bout women?"

"Can't say that she did..."

"Well, you sure learned some things pretty good someplace there, Slye. That's for sure."

"Are you talkin' about that once a month thing women get?"

Boudine erupted with a sarcastic shout, "Glory-Hallelujah!"

"What's the medicine for? You sick or somethin'?"

"No, I ain't sick. I just get the tireds once in a while and it helps get me started up, and it stops the curse from hurtin' so much."

"Where'd you come by it?"

"Calamity Jane gave me some when I got nervous a'fore doin' the first shows I was in. She got it from a Chinese show worker. Said it would stop the jitters."

"Did it?"

"Sure did. Hell, I could've gone on all day and all night."

"You use it all the time?"

"Only when I have to. Found it helps when I set out to take a stagecoach or anythin' else that might give me the jitters."

"Don't sound like somethin' that's all-fired good for ya."

"I'll be the judge of that."

"I'm sure you will..."

They both suddenly pulled up short at the sight of the tall burly long-haired bearded man, dressed in full buckskin and pelts and carrying a rifle slung in the crook of his arm. He led a mule with several beaver carcasses tied to a pack rack on its back. For a moment, it was a mutual standoff until Bob said, "How are you, sir? Name's Bob Duncan and this here's Sally Mae Boudine."

"Name of Seth Kinman from California way."

"You're a long ways from home there, Mister Kinman," Bob said.

"Heard about all the fuss and goin's on hereabouts, thought I'd come here and see for myself."

"You a miner?"

"Nossir. Trapper mostly."

"Well, I hear there's an abundance of hides here for the taking. That looks to be a Sharps Carbine you're carryin' there, Mister Kinman."

"You know your weapons there, Mister Duncan. Sharps '74 Big Fifty. You a gold miner, sir?"

"Can't say as I..."

Bob's horse suddenly snorted wide-eyed, jumped back and jerked to the side, banging into Boudine's mount. Kinman instantly raised his rifle, cocked the hammer and fired a blast that snapped past the roan and into the brush. A monstrous roar erupted. Kinman cocked the hammer again and fired a second shot at a wild thrashing in the bushes. Both Bob and Boudine's horses spooked wildly and had to be reined in. A massive dark brown grizzly bear rose up over the bushes on its hind legs, a good nine feet tall, its paws flailing in the air, its eyes rolling in terror. Kinman cocked the rifle a third time and aimed for its head, but did not pull the trigger. The magnificent specimen shivered, let out one last mournful moan, went limp, fell forward and crashed down onto the ground – mortally wounded. Kinman stepped past Bob's horse and pushed back the brush to examine the kill. "Been followin' this'ne for goin' on two days. Looks to be near nine hundred kilos, thereabouts. Should fetch a fancy price."

The bear heaved and quivered in a last death throe. Kinmen pulled his large hunting knife from the scabbard on his thick leather belt. "You folks are welcome to stay around some. I'll have this critter skinned and drawn in no time."

"Think we'll be headin' on, sir," Bob said, as he patted his horse's neck, calming the animal.

"I'll be cookin' up a real fresh liver and heart later. Ain't nothin' like it."

"We thank you, Mister Kinman, but we're lookin' to meet up with some homesteaders, if'n there are any about these parts."

Kinman stepped back and looked to Bob and Boudine, "Don't know what'yer missin'," he said with a grin.

"Thank you just the same, sir."

"I did come upon a family of 'steaders 'bout quarter day's ride up the river. Go by the name of Pickering. Good folks. Hospitable. Built themselves a good-sized cabin and are erectin' a barn and clearin' land for a farm," Kinman said.

Bob glanced over at Boudine who had stayed quiet throughout. Then, he said to Kinman, "Thank you, Mister Kinman. We'll stop by and tell them we came upon you."

"You do that. And, if you're ever over in California up near San Francisco way, just ask for Seth Kinman, they'll know where I am, and we'll raise a toast," Kinman offered with a cheerfulness that belied his appearance.

Bob raised two fingers to the brim of his *Boss of the Plains* hat and started to ease his horse forward. Kinman indicated Boudine, "She's a quiet one you got there, ain't she, Mister Duncan?"

"Not so much, Mister Kinman, not so much," Bob said with a slightly sarcastic chuckle and rode forward. Boudine nodded to the trapper and followed...

Talk was scarce between the two, as they made their way along the riverbank. Other than the crunch of their horse's hooves and an occasional warning call between game birds that danger approached, nothing much was discussed until Boudine asked, "What're you plannin' then, Slye?"

"Not sure."

"Can't see you bein' a trapper," she said, with just the hint of uncertainty.

"Not a bad life, as I can see..."

Boudine did not comment. They rode on in silence...

The chopping sounds of an ax could be heard before anyone came into view. Bob reined up on the bank of the river. Boudine pulled up as well. They listened, as the chopping sounds continued to echo through the surrounding woods. A large section of brush and trees had been cleared away, giving easy access to the water's edge. A log raft had been dragged onto the embankment, secured to a tree with a rope. There was a well-worn path from the clearing that led further inland. Bob held up his hand signaling Boudine to stay quiet, as he listened. Someone was approaching.

At the edge of the clearing, a woman stopped abruptly on the path at the sight of Bob and Boudine. It was Abigail Pickering carrying two empty water pails. They all stared at each other until Bob touched his fingers to the brim of his *Boss of the Plains* hat and nodded. "Afternoon, Missus Pickering," Bob greeted.

Abigail's face brightened, "Oh, my! It's you there, Mister Duncan. As I live and breathe. And, that be you, Miss Boudine."

"Yes, ma'am," Boudine said.

Nathan Pickering and Bob walked together, as the Pickerings' dog kept sniffing at Bob and running all around the two. They stopped about halfway between the good-sized log cabin and the several hand-hewed logs that had been erected at four corners of what was to become the Pickerings' new barn. There was a chicken coop nearer to the cabin. And, nearby, a small sod house with an added lean-to attached to a split rail fence that served as a corral and animal shelter; where the oxen and the dead highwayman's horse, that Bob and Boudine handed over to him, resided. Several goats munched on grass and shrubs anywhere they pleased. A garden, where dozens of orange pumpkins and green squashes were ready for picking, had mostly been plowed under for the coming winter. The Pickerings' covered wagon sat under the boughs of a large tree.

"That sod house there's where we hold up when we first set down the homestead."

"T'is a mighty fine cabin you've built there," Bob said.

Both Pickering children were hard at work

chopping off the limbs of felled trees with hatchets.

"I'm hopin' to get the roof on the barn before the snow."

"You've done mighty fine here, Mister Pickering."

'Nathan, Bob, Nathan... Well, we have had the Lord's blessing so far. And, the help of that Sharps rifle and that horse there. They were a godsend and we will forever be thankful to you and Miss Boudine."

"'T'was the least we could do under the circumstances," Bob said with an understanding eye toward Nathan. Then, he asked, "How far does your land extend to?"

Nathan made a wide gesture with his arm. "We registered a full parcel of 160 acres that extend far into those woods there and beyond onto the prairie. Paced it off when we first set foot here. I expect we could be farmin' a number of acres by year next, if'n our plans to grow crops for sale bear fruit. As you can see by our small garden there, the soil is rich for plantin'."

"Looks like you chose the right spot here, Nathan."

Nathan looked at Bob, then around at the land around them. "Might I ask what your plans are, Bob?"

Bob hesitated.

"Plenty of good land hereabouts for the takin'," Nathan suggested.

Bob glanced over toward the cabin, where Boudine was talking to Abigail Pickering.

"Not sure as yet," Bob said.

"Might you be thinkin' on it then?"

Bob hesitated again, then said quietly, "Yes... I be

thinkin' on it."

The lantern's glow, set in the middle of the Pickerings' table illuminated the faces of the Pickering family and their two guests who were seated with them. All of their hands were clasped in front of them and their heads bowed in prayer... All except Boudine's.

Nathan offered up Grace, "Oh, Lord, we thank thee for your mercy and your forgiveness and for the strength to endure. We thank thee for your bounty and for bringing these wonderful guests, Bob and Miss Boudine, to our table. In the name of our Lord Jesus Christ, Amen."

"Amen," they all repeated... Except for Boudine.

Nathan lifted a plate of roasted quail, took one for himself and handed the plate off to the others.

"Bob here says he might think on becoming a neighbor of ours," Nathan announced, as he took the bowl of mashed potatoes from Boudine, who almost dropped it on hearing the announcement.

"Oh, that's wonderful news," exclaimed Abigail.

Bob held up his hand. "Said only I'd think on it," he said with a bit of a nervous laugh.

The Pickerings' young son, Ben, piped up enthusiastically, "I can show you where all the best fishin' is and where to hunt deer and..."

Nathan put his large hand on Ben's arm with a smile, "I'm sure Mister Duncan will let us know if and when he decides there, Son."

Boudine looked down at her plate and stirred her mashed potatoes with her fork.

Ben asked Bob excitedly, "Can I try on your hat?"

"Ben!" Abigail admonished.

Bob smiled, "You sure can, Ben. Anyone who can hunt and fish like you deserves to wear a hat like this."

The family had set up four chairs under the night sky and gathered outside around a lighted fire pit near the front porch of the cabin. Bob and Boudine were seated next to each other, as they listened to Nathan play a lively song on his fiddle, with Abigail accompanying him on the thimble-fingered washboard. Ben wore Bob's *Boss of the Plains* hat as he danced a traditional jig with his sister, Sarah. Near the end of the song, Nathan sped up the tempo, making the children dance faster and faster until they could dance no more and collapsed in gales of laughter.

"That was real good playin' there, Nathan," said Bob, as he clapped his hands in approval. Boudine made the motions and clapped halfheartedly.

Nathan bowed his head to Bob's compliment and said, "That there was called *Soldiers Joy*. Come from the soldiers gettin' paid durin' the war so the story goes; which was told to me by my cousin, Eben Bell from up Maine way. Fought for the Union."

Sarah got up from the ground and coaxed her father excitedly, "Play the pig song! Play-the-pig-song!"

Ben joined in, "Play-the-pig-song-play-the-pig-song-play-the-pig-song!"

"Alright-alright. One more and it's off to bed with you both. You've your chores an' book learnin' in the mornin'." Then, to Bob and Boudine he said, "This one's called, *Shove That Pig's Foot a Little Further in the*

Fire."

Sarah quickly ran over in front of Bob and Boudine to clearly explain, "It ain't about a real pig," she said emphatically, "it's about a blacksmith's tool called a pig because it has tongs that look like a pig's foot."

Nathan struck a chord on his fiddle and started in. Sarah grabbed Bob's hand and started pulling him up off of his chair. "Dance with me-dance with me!" she coaxed. Bob shot Boudine a glance, then let Sarah pull him away.

Ben took the hint, ran to Boudine, and grabbed her by the hand. It took him a little longer to get her up, but she finally relented.

The fiddle played. The washboard rapped in rhythm and the dancers danced a joyful jig, as their shadows splayed up into the darkness...

The crickets were bountiful and an umbrella of stars cascaded across the crisp fall sky. The fire pit's glow still breathed out its warmth, as Bob pulled his bedroll cover over him and adjusted his head on his saddle so's to get a better look at his leather-covered notebook, where he was jotting down some notes. Boudine seemed to be already asleep in her roll nearby. Then, she uttered, "You mean to settle here?"

Bob didn't answer right off... Boudine turned and sat up. "You hear me?"

"Yes..."

"Well, you thinkin' on settlin' here then?"

"Don't know..."

"But, you really are thinkin' on it."

"Yes..."

"Thought as much."

There was silence between them for a moment, then Bob said, "You might want to think on it, as well, Boudine."

"No... don't much care for prayin' over my food all the time."

"It's a better way than gamblin' and robbin' trains and stages."

"And, near as excitin'," Boudine snorted.

Boudine rolled back into her bedroll and closed her eyes. After a moment, Bob uttered, "I told Nathan I'd stay a bit longer and help'im raise the barn frames."

Boudine was silent...

"Sure you won't stay on a bit, Boudine?"

Bob stood next to Boudine's horse, as she mounted up. She set herself into the saddle and noticeably sniffed and wiped her nose on her sleeve. "I'm goin' to see where they buried Wild Bill."

"And, get more Chinese medicine?"

"My business is my business."

"That it is, Boudine, that is is..."

"I'll be goin' then..."

Bob looked away, then back at Boudine. "Sure you won't stay a bit? They like you."

Boudine sighed and looked away for a moment, then said quietly, "Look, Slye, I told you a while back, I wasn't goin' to be tied down washin' clothes and raisin' a bunch of kids, 'member that?"

Bob looked at her for a brief moment, then answered, "Surely do."

"I stay here any longer, I might grow to like it and

then where would we be with that then?" She eased her horse around toward the path away from the homestead.

"You be stayin' around Deadwood?" he asked.

"Don't know... Might... Might not."

"Be careful then, Boudine."

She gently spurred her horse forward and away. Bob stood there for a moment, until she disappeared beyond the surrounding trees. Bob thought he might've caught a glistening in her eyes. He then turned away and walked to where Nathan was finishing skinning the bark off another tree next to where the new barn would be.

The rest of the morning was spent notching the logs, placing them in precise measurement, routing out holes and then hammering in the pegs and iron nails; making up the frames to be erected for the barn walls...

"You been rather quiet there, Bob..."

"Just a-thinkin'."

"'Bout the girl?"

"'Bout many things,"

"Well, Abigail says that too much thinkin' on things can bring on trouble."

"Could be, Nathan, could be."

"Miss Sally Mae get a look at the calendar?"

"The what?"

"The Centennial Calendar we purchased back there in Scooptown from the printer store. She was wantin' to know when the sixth of October might fall."

"Don't know. Didn't say nothin' about that."

"Think you was off in the privy 'bout that time. Anyway, be less than a fortnight away, I believe."

"Wouldn't know."

"You have any more thoughts of homesteadin' hereabouts?"

"I been thinkin' on it..."

The late afternoon sun had begun to dip overhead. Nathan stood with his hand on a large stake pounded into the ground next to a grassy field spotted with clumps of trees and bushes. Bob stood nearby as Nathan pointed to the expanse away from the stake.

"If'n you walk off the 160 acres from this point down to the river, you can get the idea of what you be lookin' at for a homestead. Cost about $18 thereabouts to register the claim. Then all's that's needed is for you to stake it off and build a small prove-up shed or drive in four stakes as to where you'd build it and then hold onto the land for five years an' it's all yourn."

"That's all?"

"That be it. But, a good moment lost might'n be found again. Hear tell, the Bohemians and the Hutterites are lookin' around these parts. Much rather it be you as a neighbor there, Bob, an' your idea of wantin' to build a tradin' post would just..."

Bob spoke up, "Just an idea there, just an idea."

"Well, we sure could use one hereabouts that's for sure."

"That'd be pretty far thinkin' on my part, I'm thinkin'."

"Well, if'n you do decide, there be a land office right in Deadwood. But, be on the lookout for one Seth Bullock. He be runnin' around buyin' up proved-up homesteads from those who can't seem to manage and want out. He just sits there and waits, then swoops in and scoops'em up like a vulture. Already made me an offer when I was only set down for a month. Told'im to go to Hades an' that the Pickerings would be here long after he saw the Pearly Gates."

Bob stopped the roan and turned in his saddle, just before riding out of sight of the Pickering homestead. He waved back at all four of the family, as they waved after him. He looked over at the straight wall frames that he and Nathan had labored together to set in place... and wondered...

Both the Wells Fargo stage driver and the guard riding shotgun acknowledged Bob, as he allowed them to rumble past on the trail coming out of Deadwood. Bob touched the brim of his hat and thought how easy it had been for him to rob a stage anytime he wanted to. The stage rolled on and Bob headed the roan along the trail, in the direction of Deadwood, South Dakota...

Bob's horse was tied to the hitching rail outside the small General Land Office in Deadwood. Inside, a clerk finished signing and stamping the homestead claim and handed it to Bob to examine. Bob paid with a twenty-dollar Gold Double Eagle and received two well-used Liberty Seated Silver Dollars in change. He touched his fingers to the brim of his *Boss of the Plains* hat and left...

As he put the document into his saddlebag, a familiar voice spoke up from the boardwalk. "Back for more writin' there, Mister Duncan?" Bob looked around. It was Sheriff Jack O'Banyon standing there grinning at him.

Bob smiled cautiously. "Well, not quite, Sheriff. Just doin' a little business."

"Homesteadin'?"

"Yessir, that be it."

"Whereabouts?"

"Belle Fourche."

"So're you stoppin' the writin' then?"

"Not exactly."

"Good. Remember, you said you'd make me famous there, didn't you, Bob?"

Bob gave an uneasy chuckle and said, "That I did, Sheriff, that I did."

Bob noticed that the sheriff was holding a handful of what looked to be wanted posters. He held one out to Bob. His eyes narrowed as he asked, "Seen anyone looked like this'ne?"

Bob took a poster and saw that the $1000 dollar reward was for a bandit whose face was fully covered with a black face scarf with eyeholes cut into it. He handed it back to the sheriff. "Can't say I've had the pleasure, Sheriff."

"Robbed the stage four days back."

Bob unwrapped his horse's reins from the hitching rail and mounted up. "Well, good-day to you then, Bob. Be careful around here. You heard what happened to old Wild Bill?" There was a sense of menace in O'Banyon's voice.

"Yessir, I did."

"Shame... Damned shame," the sheriff said with a

sarcastic smirk. "You know, they hung that little goat poker, McCall, over there in Yankton."

"Hadn't heard that."

"Yep, stretched his scrawny neck. Wished they'd let me stretch it for'im. Would'a had fun with that."

Bob touched two fingers to the brim of his hat. "Good-day, Sheriff." He reined his horse around and headed for the livery stable down the crowded, dusty, piss-puddled street.

Bob acquired a room at the Nuttal & Mann's Saloon. He looked around at the gamblers and saw not a soul who looked like Boudine, dressed as a man, at the poker tables. The new wanted poster tacked up just outside the front door was not lost on him.

He then took a stroll around the town. No sign of Boudine anywhere. Because he hadn't seen her horse at the livery, he looked into where he thought she might be gambling or eating. The printed sketch of the bandit certainly did not cast any clues in her direction. He even walked the length of the Chinese part of town, thinking she was either purchasing her 'Chinese medicine' or hiding out there. The possibility that Boudine was not anywhere to be found in Deadwood began to settle in. He was hungry and knew where to go...

At the Grand Central Hotel restaurant, Lucretia Marchbanks sat at a small window table opposite Bob, who was finishing up some of her famous plum pudding. Sadly, she spoke of Wild Bill, "I get the sadness still, when I think of him. I know the stories about the man, but there were a kindness inside that know'd no bounds.

I don't like killin', but I read in the paper that they hung Broken Nose McCall over there in Yankton and I was glad to see that he got his comeuppance."

"Did you ever see one of the shows he appeared in?" Bob asked, as he wiped his mouth on a clean napkin.

"Not the Wild West Show, but he did play a part in a western stage play sometime back that passed through here. Said he didn't like doin' it and quit. That was before he come back for good. He was married, you know."

Bob reacted with a little surprise, "I didn't know that."

"Well, didn't mind talkin' to me, but I ain't sure he spent time talkin' to other folks about it. Older woman name of Agnes Thatcher Lake out of Cheyenne, Wyoming Territory. Never did see her 'round these parts. 'Course there's those who say he was married to Calamity Jane 'fore that as well."

"He ever mention a young woman name of Boudine?"

Lucretia searched her memory, "Can't say's I recall the name."

"She used to appear in the shows dressed as a boy. Did a sharpshootin' and quick draw act."

"No, don't think he ever said nothin' 'bout that. Girl dressed as a boy you say?"

"Yes."

Lucretia stood up, as a group of customers entered. She chuckled, "I'd be sure to remember that. I hear all kinds of crazy stories that come through here. Don't pay much mind to'em." Then she remembered,

"Did hear tell there was a stage supposed to been held up by a woman bandit sometime back. Don't think much come of it 'though. You hear of that?"

"No, can't say's I have," Bob answered impassively.

"Don't seem likely does it. Well, good to see you again, Mister Duncan. Can I count on you to come back soon?"

"Appears so, Miss Marchbanks. Appears so."

She leaned over to him and said, "If'n you want to visit ol' Wild Bill, he's buried over there in Mount Moriah Cemetery. And, it's Aunt Lou to you from now on."

Standing before the grave of James Butler Hickok gave Bob a chill that he hadn't figured on. *"You never really get to know someone 'til they're gone,"* his mother used to say to him as a youngster. Not until he stood there, did he fully understand what she'd meant...

Bob lay stretched out on the single bed in the small room upstairs at Nuttal & Mann's. He had forgone any gambling and had politely declined the advances of the painted ladies in the saloon. He held out the Homestead Certificate and read it again…

It is hereby certified, ***that pursuant to the provisions of the act of Congress, approved May 20, 1862, entitled "An act to secure homesteads to actual settler on the public domain," Robert Duncan made a payment in full of Eighteen Dollars (18) in the territory of Belle Fourche, South Dakota containing 160 acres.***

Bob read the signed document again. Then, again. Then, closed his eyes...

...The stagecoach guard pulled on the brake handle as hard as he could. The driver reined in the team of horses who were wildly thrashing in their harnesses. The stage wheels locked and skidded to a stop just before crashing into the felled tree that blocked the trail. The mustached thief, with the green glasses covering his eyes, reared up on his horse with the white head marking and aimed his Winchester '73, ready to fire at anyone who showed signs of resisting. Then another bandit rode in at high speed. This one's head and face were covered with a black silk scarf with eyeholes cut into it. Then another bandit bolted from the surrounding woods. Then another, and another. Gunfire erupted. Bullets snapped in all directions. The driver stood and was riddled and ripped to bloody shreds. The guard riding shotgun raised his rifle and was blasted from his seat. Someone fired from within the coach, the stage instantly became a mass of exploding chips and splinters as the bandits' bullets ripped it apart. Then, there was silence from the stage. Not a word. Not a movement. Just the gun smoke and dust settling in the air. Suddenly, the bandits all turned and began firing wildly at each other. The sounds of exploding pistols and rifles and horses screaming in pain was deafening...

Bob awoke with a start. The shooting noise continued to ricochet off the walls of the small hotel room. He took stock of where he was and leaped from the bed to the window. The loud exploding noises were coming from the street below, as three young lads had set off a string of Chinese firecrackers and were running away from their prank. The last of the fireworks snapped. Bob stood at the window for a moment more then turned away. It was past midday and he had things to do.

Bob tore three sheets of paper from his leather-covered notebook and sharpened his Eberhard pencil. Seated at a small table near the window, he wrote the first letter that he addressed to the *Black Hills Pioneer* weekly newspaper:

Whoever I have wronged.

I am the bandit Bob Slye who robbed stages near and about and a train out of Yankton. I never killed no one. I want to give all of what I robbed back. I have told the Wells Fargo Company and the American Express Company where the money and loot are hidden. They will be going after it. If you was robbed by me you should go to the Wells Fargo Office and report it. I am truly sorry for what I have done and hope the good Lord will forgive me.

Bob Slye (Bandit)...

He then wrote a second and third letter - along with hand-drawn maps - to the Wells Fargo Company and The American Express Company and told them both where to find the hidden loot in the Wind Cave. He then pocketed the letters and left the room.

At the Deadwood Wells Fargo Office, Bob

purchased three mailing envelopes and postage stamps, addressed each and deposited them into the mail slot. He was about to leave, when he thought to ask the office agent a question, "You wouldn't by chance be holdin' any mail for Bob... I mean, Robert Duncan?"

The agent hopped down from his desk chair and went over to a wall of alphabetized wooden mail cubbyholes. His finger went to "D" and he, indeed, pulled out a small envelope and brought it back to his desk. "You be Robert Duncan?"

"Yessir, I am."

"Have any proof, sir?"

"Well, I'm known over at Nuttal & Mann's and Sheriff O'Banyon knows me and Miss Lucretia Marchbanks knows me, for sure, and before that Mister Hickok. He'd of vouched for me."

The agent looked at the letter. "Where's it sent from?"

"It would be sent from Fort Randall way..."

"That it is," the agent said and handed the letter to Bob, who took it and tipped his fingers to the brim of his *Boss of the Plains* hat and left.

Out on the plank boardwalk, Bob stood quietly and looked at the letter addressed to him. It was, most certainly, from his mother. Although, he had only seen a few examples of her writing over the years, he did recognize it as her hand. Knowing that she was not one to write letters, he figured her message must be important. He took off his hat, placed it inside the sweatband, and replaced it on his head; he would read it alone in his room.

It was at that very moment that Bob felt the woman's eyes on him. The woman seated on the buckboard. The woman in the white frilly dress. The woman name of Miriam O'Banyon. The woman who was the wife of Sheriff Jack O'Banyon...

"Good afternoon, Mister Duncan," she said softly, but with a joy and wanting in her eyes that was not lost on Bob.

Bob felt a sudden surge within him. He also felt a warning that he knew he should not ignore. "Good afternoon, Missus O'Banyon."

"Lovely day," she said, her cheeks blushing red.

"Yes, ma'am, it is that." Bob felt his own face flush and the heat filling his entire body.

"Well..." she said, "I must be heading back along the trail toward home."

Bob did not miss the lingering look in her eyes. She did not miss his look back as well.

"Good-day then," she said and flipped the reins over her horse's rump.

Bob tipped his fingers to the brim of his hat. "Good-day, ma'am. Safe travels." Their knowing looks lingered for a moment more, then she clucked to her horse and pulled away from the walkway. Bob watched, as she guided her buckboard down the street toward the end of town. Glancing back over her shoulder, not once, not twice, but three times. He quickly headed for the livery where his horse was boarded.

Every thought of warning in his head was thrust aside by the overpowering rush of passion that completely enveloped his being. As he maneuvered his horse through the heavily traveled, filthy Deadwood main street, his mind was a blur. He had already given up on ever seeing Boudine again. She had been perfectly clear that she did not want to follow his idea of registering a homestead in Belle Fourche. She did not want to *raise a bunch of kids* or *wash clothes* or *do the cookin' and cleanin'*. Even though, he thought he had seen signs that she might be thinking differently of late. But, when she saw that he was serious about registering a homestead next to the Pickerings, she had hightailed it back toward Deadwood. And, now she had disappeared from sight altogether, apparently having gone back to her old ways.

Bob rode at a fast pace, weaving in and around the outbound covered wagons and riders, who were leaving Deadwood for the day or, in many cases, forever. It didn't take long for Bob to find the side trail he had traveled before. He turned off and rode on, even though his head was filled with the words of warning that his mother had oft repeated... "*As often as you try an' make a bad idea good, it will still be a bad idea 'neath it.*" Nothing seemed to matter. Nothing could stop him. The narrow trail became a blur. He continued on until he came to the empty buckboard and horse by the thick woods where he had first encountered Miriam O'Banyon.

Bob dismounted before his horse had stopped and quickly tied the reins to a low hanging branch. He remembered the path to the grassy clearing within the woods was not a long one...

"*As often as you try an' make a bad idea good, it will still be a bad idea 'neath it.*" His boots felt as if they were walking over clouds and not touching the ground underneath him.

Then, he was there. He saw the red picnic cloth spread out on the grass beneath the thick overhanging branches that let the afternoon sun filter its warm rays down onto it. He did not see Miriam O'Banyon. Then he did, as she stepped quietly out from behind a large tree and let Bob's eyes wander over her. She was holding her white dress and undergarments in one hand and let them fall to the ground. Bob became completely overcome by her vision. She walked ever so delicately toward him, until he could feel her warm breath on his cheek... his lips... his chest, as she unbuttoned his shirt and beyond...

In that moment of ecstasy, with her body astride and writhing joyfully atop him, Bob knew in an instant what had happened when the first shot tore the flesh and bone from her left shoulder and the second sent fragments and blood splattering outward from her right shoulder. Yes, in that instant, he knew who had just fired the third bullet that smashed into her forehead and sent the back of her shattered skull flying off into the air in all directions. *King-Queen-Ace!*

ELEVEN

And, so it went.
For those two were hell-bent.
Until one fateful late afternoon...
Just before the rise of an evil Blood Moon...

Sally Mae was not a woman to be scorned.
Her discovery she much mourned...

The rifle cracked!
The .44-40 caliber smacked...
Right between the eyes of Slye's secret lover,
who rode atop in all her splendor,
astride Bob Slye's most wonderous pride...

...She was blinded by Slye's deceit.
And, after the deed was done,
she beat a hasty retreat..

Miriam collapsed down over him. Bob hastily moved her lifeless body aside and scrambled to retrieve his Peacemaker from its holster lying over his pile of clothes. He pulled the gun and jumped behind the large tree from whence Miriam had earlier appeared. He waited. Not a sound, except from his own heaving chest. His eyes darted around the woods, searching for any movement. Listening for the slightest sound of footsteps. He tasted the blood that had splattered onto his face and body. His pistol was held at the ready, but his hand was trembling uncontrollably... *'I catch you with another an' I'll cut off your...'* Boudine had said, but he had thought it was merely in jest. He peeked around the tree and saw only Miriam O'Banyon's bloody form lying motionless on the red picnic cloth. Eyes half open, staring lifelessly.

Suddenly, he made a run for it, grabbed up his boots and clothes and ran through the woods, like a rabbit running for its life from a hungry fox.

It was only after he had galloped the roan back onto the main trail and left an hour of miles between himself and the meeting place in the woods that he realized something was missing. His *Boss of the Plains* hat! It was not on his head! He reined in his horse and moved to the side of the trail to let a prairie schooner, pulled by a team of four oxen, move on through. The unopened letter from his mother was inside his hat! He would have to go back and retrieve it.

White foam formed around the roan's mouth, as Bob drove the animal hard over the miles back to where Miriam O'Banyon's buckboard and horse would be.

Bob turned the corner on the narrow trail. He saw that the buckboard was no longer there. Bob cautiously dismounted, drew his fully loaded Peacemaker and looked around. Nothing moved or made a noise. He led his horse onto the pathway toward the grassy clearing, keeping his gun cocked and ready.

The clearing was empty. Neither Miriam O'Banyon's body nor the red picnic cloth with her frilly white dress and garments were anywhere in sight. Bob stepped further into the clearing. No sign of his *Boss of the Plains* hat.

Then he heard that sound. The sound of someone cocking back the hammer of a pistol. "Figured you'd be back. This what yer lookin' for?" Came the guttural, menacing voice of Sheriff Jack O'Banyon from behind him. "Drop the gun!" But, Bob knew better. Both the Fort Randall cook, Jasper Spence, and Master Sergeant Bartholomew had taught him never to freeze when surprised. Drop low, spin and shoot. That's what he did, just grazing O'Banyon high on his left arm. O'Banyon was holding Bob's *Boss of the Plains* hat in his free hand. He instantly fired back. The bullet snapped within a breath of Bob's ear. Bob fired again in O'Banyon's direction, then again, making the sheriff duck for cover. At the same time, he swung up into the saddle and jerked the roan's reins around, jamming his spurs into the horse's flanks. The horse charged back onto the pathway. Bob turned in the saddle and fired twice in the direction of O'Banyon.

The roan bolted from the woods onto the narrow trail spitting dirt from its hooves, as it took Bob away at a full-out run, almost drowning out O'Banyon's ferocious bellow from the clearing, "I'm comin' for you! I'm comin' for you, Slye!"

Going back to Deadwood was out of the question. Possibly hiding out at Wind Cave could have worked, but he had already mailed the letter to the new *Black Hills Pioneer* newspaper and to the Wells Fargo Company, and to the American Express Company. Heading to Fort Randall would not be safe, for either himself or his mother; for her letter, now in the possession of Sheriff Jack O'Banyon, had the cancellation stamp from the fort on the envelope. Trying to lay low with the Pickerings in Belle Fourche would only bring them harm. He had left the homestead certificate in his room at the Nuttal & Mann's Saloon.

'As often as you try an' make a bad idea good, it will still be a bad idea 'neath it.'

Bob rode into the night toward the Black Hills, stopping only to water his horse and drown his own thirst at a creek. The greater the distance he put between himself and Sheriff O'Banyon, the better his chances of surviving.

The Black Hills were not unfamiliar to Bob, who had taken leave there several times, after a particularly tricky holdup. Even though they were within spitting distance of Deadwood, there were miles of canyons and caves and hostile terrain in the badlands. If luck was with him, he felt he could hold out there long enough for all of his troubles to blow over and be forgotten. However, Bob knew that luck in the game of poker was sometimes fleeting and a turn of a card could often take a gambler down...

TWELVE

...The Sheriff rode like the wind;
following the tracks of the one who had sinned.
Seething with humiliation and rage.
With only one aim –
To see the Bandit Bob Slye...
trapped in an iron-barred cage...

Silhouetted against the muted gray of early dawn, the gorges and canyons of the Black Hills loomed up on either side of Bob. Exhausted to the bone, Bob sat still in his saddle and looked back toward where he had ridden. It was quiet. Just dark shadows. Only the whispers of the constant winds that swirled in and around the ancient walls of rock. He knew that he would have to find a place to hide before dawn broke. A place where he could have a full view of the badlands, so's to spot the lone sheriff or possibly a posse that might come after him in hot pursuit.

What had possessed Boudine so much that she had to kill? I didn't know she felt like that toward me. She never said as much...

"Your ma is a strong one..."

"She is... She is that."

"She say anythin' 'bout me?"

"Just what mothers ask."

"What?"

"Nothin' special."

"She ask if I was with you?"

"Wasn't like that."

"Like what then?"

"She asked me if the good Lord would be happy about us being together..."

"Damn... She really ask that?"

"Yes..."

"Well then, Slye, d'you think he is?"

"You'll have to ask him yourself..."

She said she didn't want to raise children. She said, she'd never take a likin' to farmin'…

"This ain't goin' along with my way of thinkin' there, Bob. 'T'aint at all what I'm thinkin'."

Why?... Why then? Just because we been together all those times? She said not to think that... think that... think that...

"...You don't know much 'bout women, do ya?"

"She likes you, y'know..."

"No, she don't."

"Oh, yes... I see her lookin' at you with that look in her eyes."

"Believe me, Mother; she likes me 'bout as much as a rattlesnake likes a mongoose..."

The sun split over the horizon. Bob held the reins of the roan and led the fatigued horse on foot around a large boulder that nearly blocked the entrance to a box canyon. He would stop there. Out of sight. Ready for what he knew would come.

He checked his Peacemaker and reloaded it with the bullets from his gun belt. He then went to the scabbard on his saddle and withdrew his prized Winchester '73. He was about to check to see if the rifle was fully loaded when he noticed something off. Something very wrong. The rifle was not his. It was not his Winchester '73! His heart skipped. He flipped the rifle in his hands and knew immediately that it was heavier and that the stock was new and polished. He looked closely where the Model Number was stamped into the metal and read: *Winchester Model 1876 Centennial.* Then he saw it. The fresh engraving on the metal chamber: *To my Duncan-Dammit – Happy Birthday – October 6, 1876 – Love, S.M.B.* Bob was stunned. His head swirled. *"When's your birthday?... Everyone should know when they're born..."*

Bob flipped the lever, ejected a bullet, and saw that it was not the same rimfire cartridge that his '73 used, but was a new centerfire. On instinct, he hurriedly opened a saddlebag and there they were, two full boxes of new 45-75 caliber centerfire cartridges. He quickly reloaded the ejected cartridge, took a position behind the large boulder, and waited...

The sun began to bathe the rocky landscape in the morning light. Bob's eyes burned from no sleep. He searched for movement, but saw nothing. Then, the roan snorted loudly and began pawing the ground. Bob knew it was a warning. He pulled back the hammer on the rifle and peered over the edge of the boulder. The crack of a rifle echoed off the canyon walls a second after the lead exploded against the rock a foot from his head. Bob whirled around just in time to catch the glint of a reflection coming from the rim of the box canyon above him. The roan began to panic and pull against the reins that Bob had tied onto a small juniper tree. He aimed and fired, hitting almost exactly where the reflection had come from. Bob moved around the boulder to better shield himself. He aimed the Winchester and waited... Nothing. No movement...

Five, maybe ten minutes went by. Just an occasional hawk circling, searching for a kill. Then, from another position on the rim of the canyon, O'Banyon's voice echoed off the walls, "Hey there, Bob Slye! Won't be long 'fore you be wantin' some water there. Y'all going to get pretty thirsty 'fore long!"

Bob whirled toward the direction he thought O'Banyon's voice was coming from. In the split of an eye, he saw the glint of steel in the sun on the canyon rim, took quick aim and fired. A puff of dirt went up right near where he had intended. Again, no sound.

"Hey, Slye! Good shootin'. Nearly got me. How many bullets you got left?" O'Banyon challenged from yet another position that Bob couldn't locate.

Two lead slugs snapped by Bob's head and exploded on the boulder he was leaning against. The roan jerked back in terror, its eyes wild with fright.

"I'd say, I'm a pretty good shot there myself, wouldn't you say, Bob?" O'Banyon shouted down at him. "Just want you to know, I ain't gonna kill you straight off. I got a special plan for you, you piece of coyote shit!"

Another shot slammed into the boulder, sending a chunk of rock glancing off his forehead. Blood immediately ran down around his eye and into his mouth.

"Why'n't you make a run for it there, writer-boy? 'Course that horse of yours must be pretty tuckered out by now, an' he ain't going to be much good with a couple'a .44-40s up his ass!"

Bob wiped the blood from his eye on his sleeve and looked toward the rim of the canyon where he thought O'Banyon's voice was coming from. He squinted and saw movement several yards to the right of where he'd shot before. Slowly and carefully, he brought the new Centennial Winchester '76 up to his shoulder and sighted in, allowing for distance and windage. He chambered a cartridge, held his breath and squeezed the trigger. Then, in rapid succession, he flipped the lever-action on the rifle and fired off three more shots at the same target. He saw by the puffs of dirt that he had hit where he had aimed. He waited...

"Hey, Bob! Not bad shootin'," came O'Banyon's booming voice glancing down from the canyon rim. "Got one right through your own fuckin' *Boss of the Plains* hat!" the sheriff guffawed.

Bob flattened back onto the boulder, exasperated. He tried to chamber another cartridge, but the loading tube was empty. He realized that he had left the boxes of new cartridges further around the side of the boulder, when he had changed positions, as O'Banyon had moved. If he tried to retrieve them, he would be in plain sight of the sheriff. He set the rifle against the boulder and drew his Peacemaker. The blood from his head wound seemed to have stopped flowing and was down to a trickle. He checked his pistol. Only one bean in the wheel. Then his gun belt. Eight left in the loops. Nine bullets altogether.

"Hey, writer-boy," O'Banyon called out, "I read your ma's letter. Seems she and me are the only one's knows who you really are."

Bob gritted. He hadn't opened the letter and didn't know what his mother had written. He loaded five bullets into the Peacemaker. Three left in his gun belt...

...The sun was now overhead. He hadn't heard a sound out of O'Banyon for a time. He was parched, but his canteen was on his horse that was tied off at the juniper tree on the other side of the boulder. He slowly peered around the rock to see if he could see any movement up on the canyon rim. Nothing. Not even the wind was moving anymore. He touched the open gash on his forehead. It had crusted over and stopped bleeding. If he could get to the boxes of cartridges, he might be able to hold off O'Banyon long enough to escape. It was worth a try.

Bob edged to the other end of the boulder and stopped to listen. Not a sound. Just the sounds of the desert. He flattened himself against the rock and peered around and up toward the canyon rim. He didn't see anything, but knew that O'Banyon had him in his sights. He hunched down and looked further around the edge of the boulder, until he saw the two boxes of Winchester '76 cartridges. One opened. One closed. His body ached from lack of food, water and sleep. His head wound throbbed. The boxes were at least ten feet away. He would have to grab them and get back in a matter of split seconds.

Bob crouched, held his breath, then leaped out from behind the boulder toward the boxes. The sounds of two shots crackled off the canyon walls, after they had both hit the boxes and sent them flying, scattering the cartridges in all directions. Bob scrambled back.

"Good try there, Bob Slye. Sorry to have disappointed you," O'Banyon chortled. "Why'n't you give up an' we can both call it a day? You ain't got much left in'ya no how. Got a nice clean cell for-ya, just a few hours ride. There's water an' maybe even a hot meal waitin' for-ya. Better'n endin' up coyote food out here."

By the sound of his voice, Bob could hear that the sheriff was no longer shouting from up on the rim of the canyon. He sounded closer.

"Whudda'ya-say there, Bob?" O'Banyon called out.

Holding his Peacemaker ready, Bob moved over to the right side of the boulder, where he had left the new Winchester. It sounded as if O'Banyon had moved down onto the desert floor and was now off in that direction. Bob waited a moment, then took a glance around the rock and quickly back; hoping to draw fire. It worked. A bullet hit just above where his head had appeared. Bob saw the puff of gun smoke about fifty yards away, coming from behind a cluster of smaller boulders. He fired back. Immediately, O'Banyon returned fire, splattering the boulder with hot lead.

"Down to the old Peacemaker there, Bob?" O'Banyon called out, "That won't last'ya long."

Bob knew the sheriff was right. But, his mother had always told him, *"Whenever it seems the darkest, that's the time to rise up and fight the hardest. You might not always win, but no one can ever say you quit."*

"Hey, writer-boy? By the likes o'your mama's letter, sounds like she be a religious person. Bet she made you read the Bible didn't she, Bob?... She ever tell-ya that there's a heaven an' a hell? 'Course she did," O'Banyon laughed, "every time you was a bad little boy, she tol'ja you was goin' straight to hell, didn't she, Bob. Well, lemme tell you, this is it. This is hell and there ain't nothin' gonna get you out of it."

Bob aimed and fired his Peacemaker in the direction of O'Banyon's voice. "Shit, Bob! That was fuckin' close. Damn! How many bullets you still got left there, Bob? You'd better check, 'cause that's as long as you got 'fore I come in there and hogtie your scrawny ass," O'Banyon laughed. Bob checked the gun's chamber and loaded two bullets. One left in his gun belt.

"Ya-know somethin', Bob?" O'Banyon's voice seemed to be even closer. Bob couldn't sense exactly where it was coming from... "It ain't so much I'm mad that you killed the bitch. Hell, her time was fast approachin' with me, as it was. You just saved me the trouble... What really and truly pisses in my boots is the fact that I ain't got anyone already set aside to take over the cookin' an' the washin' an' for layin' down or for whippin' on when she gets outta line. Now, I got to go to all the fuss of catchin' an' breakin' in a whole new one."

Bob's head began to swim. He squinted up at the sun beating down on him. He heard his horse whinny for water.

"Horse of your'n gettin' fretful, sounds like.

How long 'fore it wobbles an' falls to the ground there, Slye? Buzzards could be in for a fine feed..."

There was a rustle to his left. Bob saw a shadow dart behind a crop of junipers and fired two shots. Five left altogether...

"Gettin' pretty wild there, Bob. That Peacemaker gettin' heavier in yer hand?"

"Fuck you!" Bob tried to shout, but was only able to utter a rasp whisper.

"I do believe I heard that, Bob. Bet your mama'd wash yer mouth out with lye soap she heard you talkin' like that."

His horse whinnied pathetically. Bob's breathing became short. He sat down with his back to the boulder. His eyes closed for a brief moment. He jerked himself awake, but his eyelids felt like lead weights and fluttered closed again. They snapped back open, then his pistol dropped from his hand. He quickly picked up the gun and labored to get back up on his feet. He tried to listen for a noise that would tell him where O'Banyon was hiding, but the throbbing pressure inside his head and ears made hearing almost impossible. He tried to peer around the edge of the boulder again. That's when he did hear the rustle and the click of a gun behind him. *Drop, turn and fire...* He tried, but the bullet from the sheriff's gun had already entered and torn into the shoulder muscle of his left arm. The Peacemaker dropped to the ground...

THIRTEEN

The chase finally ended in a desolate box canyon,
with a bullet lodged in his left arm.
The Bandit raised his good right hand,
signaling the end of his last stand...

With his hands tied securely to the horn, Bob's body lurched and bobbed over his saddle. Blood from the shoulder wound had drenched and dried on his shirtsleeve. As O'Banyon led Bob's horse by a length of rope tied to its reins, O'Banyon chatted on, ignoring Bob's extreme suffering.

"Well, looks like I'm the one gonna make you famous there, writer-boy."...

"Tell me, how'd you come to shoot the bitch three times then?"...

"That train you robbed over there in Yankton had two bandits. Who's the other one?"...

"Hey there, Bob, I'm gonna have me some fun with you 'fore I get the judge to sign the hangin' paper."...

"Maybe, I'll even bend you over and let ol' Deputy Pignuts have a go at'cha. How's that sound there, Bandit Bob Slye?"…

O'Banyon stopped at a creek to let the horses

drink. He drank from his canteen and held it up to tease Bob with. "Ahhhhh! Too bad, there ain't enough for you, Bob. Got a few more miles to go yet."

It was near dusk, when they approached a large tree set just off the trail back toward Deadwood. O'Banyon stopped. Bob was delirious and nearly passed out. "Hey, Bob, look up there at that big tree limb."

Bob tried to raise his head with little result. He turned just enough to squint at what the sheriff was indicating. The tree limb had eight to ten cut off hanging ropes still dangling from it. "This here's my own personal hangin' tree, Bob. If'n they think I'm gonna let them sons'a'bitches ship you off to Yankton to hang, they got another think comin'. Nope, you be mine and mine alone, writer-boy." Then O'Banyon pointed out, "See that there rope from the right, the one with the noose still on'er? That piece of dogshit was so fat that, when I jerked the horse away, ripped his fuckin' head clean off!" O'Banyon laughed aloud, then jerked the rope to lead Bob's horse off toward Deadwood...

Deputy Otis Thigpen held a lantern in the dark jail hallway as the sheriff shoved Bob forward, nearly sending him to the floor.

"Hold the sumbitch up, Pignuts," O'Banyon ordered as he took a ring of keys and opened a cell door. He then handed the keys to Thigpen, grabbed Bob by his wounded arm, and thrust him into the dark cell. "This here's your last hotel, Bob Slye. Hope you like the shit'n'piss bucket there. 'Course, don't think you got much left in'ya by now." He then said to Thigpen, "Get the bastard a bucket of water. Don't want'im dyin' 'fore I kill'im tomorrow," O'Banyon joked. Then said, "An' make sure you piss in it first," he added laughing. Thigpen locked the cell door and looked at Bob with a peculiar expression on his face - almost melancholy.

...Jessup Slye raised the whipping switch he'd cut especially for the purpose of inflicting punishment. He brought it down hard on the back of his wife, Millie Mae, out in front of the sod house. She flinched with pain, but did not utter a sound, as he thrashed her again and again. Then, Slye felt the cold tip of a rifle barrel against the back of his head and froze. "You wouldn't dare!" he blurted out. The butt of the rifle rapped hard against the back of his skull and sent him crashing to the ground. "You ever touch her again and I will kill you sure," Young Bob was heard to say...

Bob's eyes snapped open at the sounds of someone being whipped-on in the opposite cell. It was dark, except for a lantern hanging in the narrow hallway. Deputy Thigpen held tightly to a woman's slim white wrists stretched through the cell bars. From inside the cell, a drunken O'Banyon laid into her bare back, having ripped her dress down to her waist. The woman pleaded for mercy with each lash. "This'll teach you to hold money back from me, you sorry little sow!" O'Banyon shouted and lashed her again with his English leather riding crop.

"Please, I won't do it again, I promise!" the young woman implored mournfully.

"Goddamned right you won't be doin' it again!" With that, O'Banyon threw down the riding crop and drunkenly fumbled with the front of his pants. Then, roughly threw the skirt of her dress up over her back. "Hold'er tight there, Pignuts!" The Sheriff then began having his way with the young prostitute.

Bob laid his head back down on the wooden bench he was sleeping on and tried to block out the violence being forced upon the poor woman.

"Hey, writer-boy? You awake in there? You see this?" O'Banyon shouted out to Bob. "This's about as close as yer gonna get to a lay, 'fore I set the rope around yer scrawny neck," he laughed as he finished and buttoned up his pants. He then, stumbled out of the cell and stood weaving next to the bars looking in at Bob. "See you early in the mornin'. Judge be comin' here to sign the execution paper." He laughed again and walked unsteadily down the hallway. Thigpen let go of the prostitute's wrists and locked her cell door. Bob thought he heard the deputy whisper, "I'm sorry," but couldn't be sure.

As Thigpen turned to leave, he stopped and stood right up next to the bars of Bob's cell. "Sssst!" Bob heard and looked up. The deputy looked toward the end of hallway for a moment, then carefully reached into his pocket and retrieved a small leather pouch. He quickly flipped it into the cell and whispered, "Woman said you'd know how to use this."

"What woman?" Bob managed to ask in a hoarse whisper.

"Don't know. Brown dress and a long bonnet coverin' up her face." ... *Boudine!'...*

"Hey, Pignuts! Get yer cockleburred ass in here!" O'Banyon shouted from the front office. Thigpen turned and hurried away.

With not much strength to call on and with his left arm nearly useless, Bob retrieved the leather pouch and opened it. It contained yarrow grind. There was a ladle in the water bucket. Bob dipped a little water and mixed the yarrow into a paste, scooped it out of the ladle bowl and pressed all of it into his shoulder wound. He was so numb all over; he could barely feel the pain. He then put the pouch into his pocket and laid down on the bench, falling dead asleep...

"Don't think about it! Get the fuck up, you piece of cow dung! Rise'n'shine!"

FOURTEEN

They gave Bob Slye a quick-justice trial.
He stood through the judgment with nary a smile.
For the Bandit knew only too true;
that he was responsible for his own Waterloo.
The Judge never asked and Slye would never tell,
that it was she and not he,
who had delivered the Sheriff's wife to her own eternal hell.

Bob stood in the sheriff's office with both hands shackled in front of him. With the morning sun blasting through the front window, O'Banyon appeared to be a looming silhouette against the bright light. Seated behind the sheriff's desk was the Justice of the Peace Roy Raintree. He seemed disinterested, as he looked off through the window at nothing in particular. O'Banyon tossed three items onto the desk. "These was found in his saddlebags. One black mustache. One set of green glasses and this white paint he used to disguise his horse." He then unfolded a wanted poster with the sketch of the Bandit Bob Slye and set it on the desk as well. "Goes along with this poster that was sent out from over Scooptown way."

The judge fiddled with the items with a beefy

hand and uttered, "Anythin' else?"

O'Banyon picked up an envelope set out on the front of the desk and took out a letter. "This here's a letter from this bandit's mother. Says who he is." He started to hand it to the judge.

Raintree waved it away, "Read it," he said to O'Banyon.

O'Banyon adjusted his reach and read from the letter...

Dear Son

I am not so good at leter writin. But I am worrin about you. Mr. Bartholomew showd me the poster with the name of Slye. It be the likness of your Pa Jessup Robert Slye. He was a bad man lost in the drink. He were a gamblr and robber. He used the name of Bob Slye with othr bad foks. He nevr read the Bible He only read the Devils book. The man in the pitcher looks like him but he was kilt by another of his kind. I hop this leter gets to you and you are safe. I love you son dont never forget that. Rember that the Lord keeps a list and ther is always time to make it good.

Mother

Judge Raintree closed his eyes for a moment, then gave Bob a slow, disinterested glance. "Your name be Robert Slye?"

Bob uttered hoarsely, "Yessir."

"These be yours?" the judge asked, indicating the items on the desk.

Bob nodded with difficulty, "Yessir..."

"You killed and shot dead a woman name of Miriam O'Banyon?" he asked, as he gazed out the window. Bob didn't answer. The judge slowly looked back at him and repeated, "You killed and shot dead a woman name of Miriam O'Banyon?" Bob still did not answer. Justice of the Peace Raintree's face began to redden. He fingered O'Banyon's riding crop laying on the desk to his right. "I'll ask you one more time, son..." He then grabbed up the riding crop and snapped it down hard on O'Banyon's desk, shouting, "Did-you-kill-the-sheriff's-wife?"

Bob took a deep breath and answered very quietly, "Yessir."

Without speaking any further, the judge took up a pen, dipped the nib into the inkwell at the front of the desk, and scratched his signature onto the court order in front of him. He then turned the paper in O'Banyon's direction and handed him the ink pen. Sheriff O'Banyon dipped the pen into the inkwell and affixed his signature. Judge Raintree opened a leather holder, took out a cast iron Official Court Embosser and crimped the order over his name.

Quietly, and without ever setting his eyes on Bob again, he gathered up his things and left the office, just as Deputy Thigpen came rushing in.

"Where the hell've you been?" O'Banyon shouted.

Thigpen stuttered, "I been-I been-I been..."

"Jesus Christ, Pignuts, you sound like a damned parrot! I need you to get your puckered ass out to the tree and tie on a new hangin' rope."

"Yessir-yessir..." Thigpen gave Bob a look...

"Now!" O'Banyon roared.

The deputy turned tail and headed for the door. "Use the wagon an' have the coffin ready when we get there," he shouted after him.

"Yessir," Thigpen yelled back as he hurried down the boardwalk...

It was nearing high noon. O'Banyon led Bob's roan along the trail toward the hanging tree, with a rope tied to its reins. Bob was expressionless, his hands secured to the saddle horn.

"Too bad about that homestead of your'n there, Bob. Found the certificate in your room over at Nuttal & Mann's. Plannin' on goin' on over to Belle Fourche to see if it's worth provin' up. If it is, I'll make a split offer to a new man in Deadwood name of Seth Bullock. He's a smart sumbitch, with money and a good eye for land hereabouts. I be killin' two birds with one stone. What've you to say on that, Slye?"

Bob didn't answer. "Cat got your tongue there, Bob?" O'Banyon chuckled. "Guess so. Time for you's near up." Then, he asked, "What the hell's all that writin' in that leather-covered book of your'n? Tried to read it. Couldn't make head nor tail out of it. Just a bunch of hen scratch... Don't matter no how where you're goin' anyway, do it, writer-boy."

Bob lifted his head to see where they were on the trail. There was a fall chill in the air. O'Banyon had put on a sheepskin jacket to ward off the cold. Bob was wearing the same blood stained garments that he was captured in. The binds around his wrists throbbed.

"Almost there, writer-boy. I'd ask you to go fishin' with me later, but I hear you'll be shovelin' coal somewhere else." O'Banyon chuckled at his own joke. Then he carried on with, "You ever run up against a woman bandit out there? Hear tell she struck again t'other week."

Bob didn't answer. He glanced around at the rolling hills spotted with clumps of trees, but saw nothing.

"Can't believe there'd be a fuckin' woman with the gumption to rob a stage. World's gettin' stranger an' stranger all the time." Then he said to Bob, "Look, Slye, there's the hangin' tree up ahead. Looks like ol' Pignuts's got it all ready for-ya. Maybe the little sheep-poker did somethin' right for once."

Deputy Thigpen moved the ladder he'd used to climb up to the limb to tie off the new noose. O'Banyon led Bob's horse just under the dangling rope loop. He then circled his own horse to the rear of the wagon that Thigpen had used to haul the wooden coffin to the hanging tree. As O'Banyon dismounted, he ordered, "Pignuts, cut'im loose from the saddle horn there and tie his hands tight." Thigpen pulled a hunting knife from the scabbard on his belt and did exactly as he was told. What the sheriff did not see was the eye contact the deputy had with Bob that told him something was in the wind.

The sheriff took the English riding crop he had brought with him and stepped up onto the wagon, then he maneuvered the horse to bring it right up alongside Bob. "See this box we got here 'specially for you, Bob?

'Bout ten minutes you be in it, then Pignuts there'll be haulin' you back to Boot Hill and puttin' you in the ground for good," O'Banyon said with a salacious grin. "Still think stickin' your pickle in that bitch was worth all this fuss there, Bob? Shit, just think, you could be off in Belle Fourche provin' up a new homestead, 'stead'a bein' out here chokin' for air on the end of that there rope."

Bob looked straight ahead, shifting his eyes from right to left. There was nothing more than the cold gray sky and the rolling hills with the clumps of trees dotting the prairie. The Black Hills loomed off in the distance.

"Never give up hope... There's always hope on the horizon, when all hope seems the darkest." His mother's words of wisdom came to him, as O'Banyon ordered, "Alrighty, Pignuts, put the bag over Bob's head here so's we can get on with it."

Deputy Thigpen froze for a moment, then stuttered nervously, "I... I... I din't bring it..."

O'Banyon's eyes widened and his face grew red with rage. "You din't bring it?" he seethed. Then, he almost whispered, "Come 'ere, Pignuts..." Thigpen seemed frozen to the ground. "I... said... come 'ere you little rodent." The deputy stepped toward the wagon and stopped within a yard. "Closer," O'Banyon ordered with a gold-tooth smile. Thigpen took another step closer. "Closer, now..." Thigpen's eyes were wide with fear. He inched a half step nearer. "Come on now, I ain't gonna hurt'ya..." Thigpen stepped up right next to the wagon where O'Banyon stood over him, passively smiling. In a sudden move, O'Banyon brought the leather crop viciously across the deputy's face, breaking the skin. "You little bag of pig vomit! I should make you get right in that there box with'im an' nail you up an' bury you alive myself!" Then, the sheriff turned toward Bob, grinning, "Damn! Looks like we have'ta watch your tongue waggle and yer eyes pop out there, Bob. Then he glared at Thigpen and ordered evenly, "Get up an' put the rope on'im. See if you can do that right."

With blood oozing from the lash across his cheek, Thigpen hurried around to the other side of Bob's horse to move the ladder to the limb. He climbed to where he could reach the noose. His hands shook uncontrollably, as he took the loop and attempted to put it over Bob's head. He had to take it back to loosen it to fit.

"Jesus Christ, Pignuts! What the fuck's wrong with you today? You done this a hundred times 'fore. Now, get to it, goddammit!"

Thigpen loosened the noose and unconsciously seemed to look around, as if waiting for someone or something to happen. As he finally placed the noose around Bob's neck his eyes glistened. "Tighten'er up real tight," O'Banyon ordered. "Don't want to hav'ta do it again."

Thigpen tightened the noose some, stepped down off the ladder and moved it away. Standing on the wagon bed, O'Banyon moved to within striking distance of the roan's rump and nonchalantly slapped the riding crop on the palm of his hand. "Well then, Bob Slye the Bandit, got any last words? Not that it'll do you any good."

Bob looked straight ahead. Thigpen looked down at his boots with his hands folded in front of him.

"Well, here we go. Say hello to the Devil for me,"

O'Banyon said gleefully and raised his riding crop high over the roan's rump...

The bullet ripped through the sheriff's right shoulder, shattering the joint in a burst of blood and bone. Thigpen quickly grabbed the bit of Bob's horse to steady it. The crack of the rifle shot echoed across the expanse, as a second shot followed and blew O'Banyon's left shoulder away. Bob didn't have to try to look, as he heard the third bullet blast through the sheriff's skull, followed by the echo of the gunshot ricocheting off into the distance. *'King-Queen-Ace'*...

O'Banyon tipped back in a dead fall right onto the wooden coffin with a heavy thud. Thigpen quickly moved the ladder back and hurriedly removed the noose from around Bob's neck and cut away the bonds on his wrists.

"She done what she said," Thigpen told Bob, as he stepped off the ladder and climbed up into the wagon. The deputy looked down at the still form of the dead sheriff and drew his gun. He slowly bent down and placed the barrel of the weapon onto the man's chest over his heart. Cocked the hammer back and calmly pulled the trigger. Thigpen straightened up and holstered his gun. "Better late than never. Would've done it anyway... one of these days..."

Bob sat dazed with this sudden turn of events. He scanned the hills, but saw not a movement there, or anywhere. Thigpen rolled O'Banyon's body off the coffin and removed the loose wooden slab top. He reached in, pulled out a full carpetbag and Bob's new Winchester '76 rifle, and lastly, his *Boss of the Plains* hat with the bullet hole right through it. "Brought all your belongings along, so's you won't have'ta go back into town." Then, a big grin of relief spread across the deputy's face, "Less'n, you wants to be at your own buryin'. "

Bob finally found some words, "How'd you know to..."

Thigpen answered, as he went about the business of tugging and lifting the heavy body of O'Banyon into the coffin and nailing the wooden lid down tight. "The woman, tol' me how it was an' how it could be for me."

"She pay you?"

"Some, but that don't matter. Like I say, this day was comin'. She just brought it on. Guess it t'was the right time for you, Mister Slye."

"Duncan. The name's Duncan."

"Yessir, that be right. But' it'll be the Bandit Bob Slye writ over this here coffin, that's for sure."

Thigpen got down off the wagon and took Bob's belongings to him. He then unhitched the sheriff's horse, set the reins over the saddle horn and slapped it hard on the rump. The horse bolted into a gallop and sped away across the prairie. "Now, you best be gettin' on there, Mister Duncan," Thigpen said, as he handed up Bob's hat to him. "There seems to be someone waitin' yonder fer-ya."

Bob looked toward a clump of trees atop a rise and saw the silhouette of a rider waiting. He recognized it to be Boudine. Bob placed the *Boss of the Plains* hat on his head and touched his fingers to it in a salute. "Thank you, Otis... 'Til we meet again..."

"Yessir," Otis Thigpen replied, smiling. "'Til we meet again... someday..."

Sensing the excitement and direction he should head, the roan reared up on its hind legs and pawed at the air. Bob grabbed his *Boss of the Plains* hat from his head and waved it to Otis. The roan then twisted back down to the ground and broke into a full-on gallop, kicking up clouds of dust, as they rode away, leaving Deadwood far behind...

FIFTEEN

Some say, Sally Mae Boudine was never heard from anymore.
Some claim, she'd wound up just another frontier whore.
But, that seemed unlikely for a wild one such as she.
Because, she was a she...
Woe-is-me...

There is a lonely grave up on Boot Hill,
Where HERE LIES THE BANDIT BOB SLYE is chiseled in rotting wood.
Atop a mound that only they understood.
The story goes that he'd swung from the gallows holding his story true.
Because, even for a bandit, it was the honorable thing to do.

Ol' Bob Slye was the apple of his mother's eye...
But, a bandit he would be.
And, hangin' with the truth...
Was the only way to finally set him free...

...Or was it?

ACKNOWLEDGMENTS

The editing stage of writing a book can be a rather tortuous journey. Turning over a completed first draft to someone else takes complete trust. That's what Melinda Riccilli Slade brings to the process. That, and a cure for the comma-crazed and the exclamation point addicted.

With this subject matter, I was pleasantly surprised that this book passed muster on the first read-through and the focus went directly to typos, spelling, punctuation and simplification of some self-indulgent character overwriting.

So, it is with deep appreciation that I thank Melinda for her dedication, organizational skills, hard work, experience and critique in helping to bring this novel to its fruition.

I also wish to thank Morgan Riccilli Slade, once again, for his imaginative cover creation. He really caught the essence of the story.

Thank you, Mitchel Slade, for your encouragement and energy, and for creating such a unique work environment.

A very special thank you to all of my readers for their kind words and support for my efforts.

ABOUT THE AUTHOR

Mark Slade is an author, artist and actor. HANGIN' WITH THE TRUTH is his second novel. His first novel, GOING DOWN MAINE was set in New England, where he grew up. He also authored two books of poetry and art. Combined with his illustrations and photography, OF PAIN AND COFFEE and SOMEONE'S STORY reflect his unique perspective on everyday life. He lives in Northern California with his wife, Melinda.

For Additional Biographical Information:

www.marksladestudio.com
www.imbd.com
www.wikipedia.org
Facebook
Twitter